W9-BSN-491

First edition published in 2001 by
Zoland Books, Inc.
384 Huron Avenue
Cambridge, Massachusetts 02138

FIRST EDITION

Book design by Boskydell Studio
Printed in the United States of America

05 04 03 02 01   8 7 6 5 4 3 2 1

This book is printed on acid-free paper, and its binding
materials have been chosen for strength and durability.

Library of Congress Cataloging-in-Publication Data
Spitzer, Mark, 1965–
Chum / Mark Spitzer.
p.   cm.
ISBN 1-58195-031-4
1. Survival after airplane accidents, shipwrecks, etc. — Fiction.
2. Motion picture actors and actresses — Fiction. 3. Islands — Fiction.
4. Alaska — Fiction. 5. Black humor (Literature) gsafd I. Title
PS3569.P558 C48 2001
813'.6 — dc21   00-067309

ACKNOWLEDGMENTS

Chum is based on a short film sketch by the French novelist and infamous polemicist Louis-Ferdinand Céline, to whom I owe my major inspiration for this novel. Céline's idea, entitled "Secrets dans l'île," was first published by Éditions Gallimard in 1936 in an anthology called *Neuf et une,* and it later appeared in the collected works. With some assistance from the translator Simon Green, veteran writer in residence at Shakespeare and Company in Paris, I translated "Secrets" into English in the winter of 1995. The plot revolved around a bunch of jealous islanders off the coast of Brittany who are driven to shocking acts of violence. In liberally adapting the characters and setting, however, I added details that had never been intended or envisioned by Céline.

For example, I chose to place the action in Alaska on the advice of the underground filmmaker Lars Larsen, who deserves some credit for this book. Back when I was adapting my translation into a screenplay (years before it became a novel), Lars and I drove an Impala across America, discussing mechanics of the plot. These discussions affected the evolution of *Chum,* and I thank Lars for his input on this project, especially in regard to Alaskan fish.

Likewise, I'd like to thank the following people, who were helpful in the development of *Chum:* Laura Rosenthal, for selecting the original translation ("Secrets on the Island") for *Exquisite Corpse 60;* Paul Spitzer and George Whitman, who provided me with places to stay in my transient days working on the screenplay; Peter Foldy, for cinematic interest and advice on audience empathy; Robin Becker, for dialogue about the characters — not to mention moral and immoral support; Andrei Codrescu, whose comments on pace and voice were pivotal; the entire and unnameable graduate Fiction Workshop at LSU in the spring of 1999 (especially Rex Rose, who came up with the title, causing us both to roll on the floor laughing hysterically), for invaluable remarks later incorporated into the revision; and everyone at Zoland Books, for putting this book together.

I am also grateful to the literary journal *murmurs,* which published excerpts of this work, and *Exquisite Corpse,* which ran this novel in serial form.

Finally, I'd like to acknowledge the lowly bottom feeders of the Pacific Northwest (particularly Puget Sound, which the fish of this fiction are based on) for capturing my imagination and holding it since I was six. I was introduced to these creatures by my father, and for this, and other things as well, I dedicate this book to him.

— Mark Spitzer
Baton Rouge
2000

chum, *n.* 1. [from *chamber fellow.* Cf. comrade] A room-mate, as in a college; also, an intimate friend; habitual companion; associate. *Now colloq.* 2. [origin obscure] Chopped fish, fish blood, or the like, thrown overboard to draw fish. 3. Refuse or scrap fish, as in a fish cannery; also, the pulp left after expressing oil from menhaden. *U.S.* 3. *v.i.* To fish with the aid of chum, chopped fish, or viscera. 4. *n.* The common dog salmon (*Oncorhynchus keta vulgaris*).

CHUM

I

LO: AN ISLAND SO far north and so far removed from the Alaskan mainland that it is almost Russian — way way out in the Bering Strait, in the steel gray spray, beneath the dirty dingy oceanic sky, in the swirling fog and breaking waves where the ice of the Arctic comes screeching down like a host of hags to freeze in the beards of fishermen, who are used to coughing, flu, phlegm, and the monsters they haul from the blue-black depths: grotesque bubble-eyed cod, great skates, half-ton halibut, gothic sculpin, cabezone, and all the bullheads and rockfish and dogfish and ratfish they know — which they take back to their island that doesn't even have a name, just a cannery, a trailer park, a market, a bar, some summer homes, a school, a church, roads in disrepair, a power plant, a gas station, and the high cliffs and beaches surrounding this rock — where ships from Russia, Japan, Canada, and the States stop for fuel, then leave this place where men fish and fight and fuck and the women work in the cannery wearing slate gray smocks splattered with the blood of creatures brought in bins and spread out on the slime line, where they're gutted and cleaned and processed into dog food.

These women have been together so long, and have worked together so long, that their bodies are attuned to each other. Once a month, the cannery becomes a dim fluorescent menstrual hut, where the salt air hums with a tension as thick as the mist in the bay. Sometimes a life is lost in the cogs, or the pistons of machinery, but nothing ever comes of this. And it's the same at sea, where the elements strike randomly. There is no law enforcement here, just a post office, a company story, and a graveyard. Fifty is the average age, seventy-two is the oldest. The young are rare, and the main cause of death is suicide. Rape is the norm — that's how people are born.

Up the hill, at the highest point on the island, there's an iron cross on top of the church, attached to a cable strung to a pole driven into the earth. Here, lightning strikes every winter, sometimes ten or twenty times per day. It is almost always raining.

In March the storms reach biblical proportions. The sky billows black from morning to night like some all-consuming mushroom cloud held in, sometimes blowing in at a hundred miles per hour, looking like the depths of hell erupting from some rupture and roiling with the wrath of God searching for a Sodom or Gomorrah to smear.

There are tendrils in the turbulence, detonations, and gulls tumbling in flight, feathers snapping, wings ripping, necks twisting. It's a storm that comes every year, smashing boats, sinking ships — it rides the skyline, right above the waterline, which rises to meet it, foaming and frothing, lifting and breaking, then churning into waves that crash down on each other with hundreds of tons of pressure — where the unlucky have clung to whatever they could, no sense of gravity or direction in that space of chaos where water and weather rush together, roaring toward the island in the shape of a comma half the size of Iowa. There's nothing to do but batten down the hatches.

The people of the island, however, are not afraid of this storm; it is part of their life and just as expected as birth and death. The plywood goes up and the anchors go down. The cannery is the safest place in town, a concrete cube with cinder-block walls. The women go to work and the men stay at home, sleeping or drinking or beating their kids. Though some men go out, with nets and traps and buckets of chum, but not because they're braving the storm. They never know where the tempest will form, or if it will even hit the island. Sometimes it misses, and then a day's catch is lost from laying low. Other times, though, the town must be repaired. In any case, the resource they depend upon is always worth more than the lives of a few measly men, who are disposable and paid by the pound — as are the captains, who make the decision when to go out and when to come in.

Such is the scene one morning in late March: the women are scrambling to get to work, the school bus is unloading in the darkening dawn, and the sun is coming up somewhere beyond the hovering clouds. It's one of those days that could go either way; the horizon is low and the sky's not getting any lighter. It could hit that afternoon, it could hit in a week. The town is preparing; hammering can be heard on every street. Shattering glass is a pain in the ass.

Five boats took off before dusk, two have already come

back. The captains have either chickened out, caught their catch, come to their senses, or they're dead. They always cut it close.

It isn't raining but the wind is picking up. A strange green glow can be seen in the foam. The tide is rising, lapping at the driftwood left last year. Every time the tide recedes, dead fish — or nearly dead fish — are left on the beach. Some are already rotten, smelling sweet and fetid, attracting flies. Others are buried under kelp. Man-o'-wars are everywhere, their orange and yellow streamers coated with sand and pieces of white shell.

Out on the spit, over a thousand Ping-Pong balls have just washed up — for a reason that no one here will ever know. They bounce and roll and float between the barnacled masses lodged in the sand: rusty axles, mufflers, tires. Puddles of oil also wash up, with shreds of netting, litter, logs. Then an eel appears, six feet long, half-devoured by the crabs. Then a salmon, gasping.

An albatross swoops down and stands on the sand, amidst the flipping fingerlings. Spray begins to blow toward the land. A dead dog washes up, bloated like a buoy, its fur worn off. It hits a piling, punctures, and slowly deflates. Another boat comes in, its flag at half-mast.

Over by the rocks, a seal pops up, swimming toward the musseled caves. Rain can be seen a few miles out, thicker in some places, thinner in others — but nevertheless coming closer. Crows begin to call to each other, a dog starts to howl. Others answer. Their communal cry hangs in the air. Doors swing open and fishermen come out, kicking at curs and yelling, "Shut the fuck up!" It doesn't do any good. A gunshot goes off. Somewhere, a dog lies dead as a man goes back to bed. But the baying does not cease.

Now the waves are getting higher, and there is even more garbage blowing in: Russian wrappers, Canadian cans, bottles, diapers, pieces of paper. It all ends up caught in the kelp. More and more fish wash up. Some have been dead for days, but the eyes of most are just starting to film over. Every time a wave rolls in, hundreds of fish are left in the sand: sand dabs, sea perch, tomcod, ling.

The gulls descend and rip into flesh. There are thousands of gulls lifting and diving and swooping along the beach. They are in a frenzy, tangles of intestines bloodying their breasts. Like buzzards, they fight each other, even though the spoils are everywhere. Birdshit splatters, rain descends.

Another boat comes in, and then a wall of water hits. Sheet rain slams the beach so hard that gulls fly squawking back to the cliffs, but only some of them make it. When a raindrop hits the sand, it forms a crater larger than an egg. The sand starts to shift and writhe with a texture just as alive as the water. A rumbling comes closer.

The dogs are all inaudible now, hunkering under trucks, stairs, stoves, each other. Only the armored venture outside.

They come up from the sea and down from the rocks, emerging from crags, tide pools, grass. There are thousands of them: brown, red, blue, green. Covered with limpids, barnacles, kelp: snow crabs, spider crabs, red rock, Dungeness — feasting on the smorgasbord, gnashing claws, clicking, scratching, scavenging. They climb each other, carpet each other, consuming the entire beach, tearing at the meat. In some places, the sand is knee-deep in crab.

The crab masses devour. The rain beats down. The roaring increases. The ocean lifts — then descends, smashing their backs. Thousands are sucked under, then spat up again. Shells splinter, pincers are ripped out. Trees wash up. A life preserver, faded yellow by the sun. Human waste. Styrofoam chunks. And then the battered gulls arrive, half of their feathers torn away, slapping down on the crabs, rolling in the sand, freshly dead — a belt of them, forty or fifty or sixty miles long, pushed ahead by the tide. It's coming.

Lightning strikes the cross on the church. Once, twice — thunder booms, hail smashes down in lug-nutlike conglomerations, bouncing off the docks, cascading on the roofs. Pigs get hit and die on the spot. The noise carries through the harbor like machine-gun fire, sounding the first barrage of the storm. But suddenly, it's gone and replaced by sleet. Plants break under the weight, the streets are instantly glazed.

And then it appears eighteen miles out: complete blackness, rising higher and darker than anything anyone here has ever seen. Church bells start to clang: *Emergency! Take cover! Stay away from windows! Pray to God, Motherfuckers!*

The islanders know what to expect. The power will go out and the blackness will take over. Things will get hit by mysterious missiles, and gutters will gorge, forcing pressure into homes. Toilets will erupt, so are duct-taped shut. Buckets will be used. And mops and rags and barrels and drums. Rain will burst in. Destruction is a given. People will be injured, maimed, killed. Livestock is doomed. And when it all blows over, there will be fish in the streets, uprooted trees, overturned cars, trailer homes floating out to sea, and school will be canceled. But before the cleanup begins, the whole town will go to the beach to reap what God has given them.

2

ROM OVER THE DUNES, they descend like the hag
masses of the seventeenth century, actually cack-
ling, laughing, jumping, and running, armed with
sacks for plunder. Most of them are women, many of them
toothless, all of them squarish and squat. Descendants of
Irish criminals, they retain in their genes a nuance of
Down's syndrome thanks to a century and a half of vigor-
ous inbreeding.

Back when Australia was the New Welsh Prison Colony,
an English prison hulk known as *The Ophelia* was set upon
by Mongolian pirates off the coast of Borneo, so it fled up
the Makassar Strait, where a winter storm blew it into the
Pacific. The ship got lost but eventually found its way to
the Russian coast, where another storm hit, busting the
mainmast in half and shredding the sails to gauze. *The
Ophelia* was soon beached on an island a quarter of a globe
away from its original destination. The captain, however,
decided that one rock in the middle of nowhere was just as
good as any, so he dumped his cargo there. Repairs were
made, and the hulk sailed back to England the long way,

around Cape Hope. There were several mutinies and it took a few years. When they finally returned, the queen made it known that such an embarrassing and wasteful circumnavigation never occurred. The details of the voyage of *The Ophelia* were hidden from history, and the islanders were left to their own devices.

Because they are a pretty much illiterate people, there are no written records on how the place was settled, and nobody here gives a damn to know. They just fish and work and speak with a slightly Irish accent, which is bent by a Danish inflection due to commerce with whalers in the early 1800s, when the Scandinavians came for the trade of blubber — which became the mainstay of the people well into the next century.

The general population of the island didn't even know they were under American jurisdiction until the middle of the 1960s, when they found out they had been sold to the United States along with Alaska. They discovered this because of the post office, which was set up when a big oil company was forced to clean up a spill in the area, and so established a port to pretend their workers were doing something other than getting drunk and partaking of the local loins. If it wasn't for the whorehouse erected in '64 (when the men discovered they could pimp their women instead of slaughtering whales), the blue sperm whale would now be extinct.

Following a scourge of syphilis, an exponential rise in birth defects, and a generation of mental retardation, the company store and cannery were founded by the great-grandson of Chief Seattle, who brought industry to the island — which experienced its prime in '66 with the paving of some roads because of demand for a ferry. The town, however, never developed into the resort the ferry was built for because the developer, a Nazi war criminal, was exposed, then bludgeoned to death on the streets of London. When the oil company left in '72, the whorehouse lost its business and the people were forced to concentrate on fishing again. Jimmy Seattle made a bundle by switching from salmon to garbage fish — which is the local term for bottom feeders, a class of fish that isn't good for much except grinding up, packing into cans, and labeling dog food. Since then, the townsfolk have been subsisting mainly on cod, workmen's comp, and social security. This is the history of the island.

In the distance, church bells are ringing. It is a sedated day, much warmer than the day before, the storm having blown through the night while the men slept drunk and the women prayed for the bounty of this day. Like last year, and the year before, and all the years they can remember, the misfortune of others is no tragedy for them. It is exactly the opposite.

Dressed in gray like the after-storm sky, varicose veins race across the sand, occasionally stooping to scoop up a duck, twist its neck, then throw it in a sack, or grab a fish if it is still fresh. The sun has just come up, and it is payday on the island.

Some children tag along, skipping and hopping and scanning the sand. Few in this crowd, however, are under thirty. Nadine is an exception to the rule. In comparison to the rest, she is almost beautiful. Down in Juneau she probably wouldn't turn any heads, but she might get a job as a stripper. She is nineteen, carries a couple defective genes, has been abused by her father, neglected by her mother, and has no ambition except to get laid by someone who is not a family member.

Nadine dresses like the rest but hides her face in a heavy scarf and her body in a frumpy coat. To show one's youth on the island is a sin, and it can get you raped and beaten. But even worse is the treatment she'd receive from the women if she didn't try to hide her skin, not yet plagued by wrinkles and age.

A Canadian honker appears at her feet. She stoops and grabs it as someone slaps her on the ass. Nadine looks up and sees old One Eye rushing by, still drunk and weaving in the sand, his hand grasping the shape of her butt. Once she sucked him off, but only because her father made her. Like most of the men on the island, he is fat, with bad breath, and has too much hair on his body and face. Nadine despises beards.

She looks at the goose. It is still alive with two broken wings. How it got here, she'll never know. They usually fly south for the winter.

"Stupid bird," she tells it and starts to crack its neck. For a second, though, the goose stares up with pleading eyes, and for a second she hesitates. But Nadine has learned to get past that. This goose is dinner. *Snap!* She throws it in the bag.

On the beach a yacht has washed up. It is smashed all to hell and surrounded by clothes, dishes, furniture, and ravens.

The crowd tops the dune, sees this, cheers as one, and descends upon the wreck. The ravens lift into the sky, airing their discontent. According to the stern, this vessel is from Santa Barbara and is dubbed *Pacific Dream*.

Stumbling and lurching, the women gather what they can, while the men board the craft looking for liquor. Nadine throws her finds in with the goose: some silverware, a fancy ashtray, string, a spool of thread, a spatula, and a makeup case — which she quickly opens, then snaps shut and throws in the sack. There were all sorts of lipsticks in there, and things that only a whore would wear — that is, according to Mother Kralik, who tells the women what they should believe. And that's what they do believe. Nadine looks around.

Father O'Flugence is in the distance, watching the people scouring the wreck. For a second Nadine feels a sheepish tweek but then remembers he is always there when a boat washes up, and it's not like he doesn't take a little for the church. She knows he knows what happens to survivors, if there are any. And she knows he knows that God knows. Father O'Flugence is a sorry old fuck. She sees him kneel and pick something up.

Meanwhile, Mother Kralik is coming closer, scavenging the sand. She picks up a goblet, sneers at it, drops it into her bag, then goes for a cup with a picture of the Eiffel Tower on it. Nadine takes a step back.

If Mother Kralik passes by and doesn't see her, that will be just fine. Mother Kralik, the oldest woman on the island, gives Nadine the creeps. "The bitch is a witch," according to Nadine's mother, and Nadine doesn't doubt it.

Mother Kralik lives at the end of the road, where animal skulls mark her shack, a place Nadine has been before, but not by choice. Nadine's mother used to take her there whenever she had a fever. But she never recovered because of Mother Kralik's "medicine"; she always recovered because kids recover — or else they die.

Nadine hated Mother Kralik's foul concoctions, which always made her gag. And she hated the way that one yellow tooth would always shine with saliva. Nobody on the island had very good teeth, but Mother Kralik's were the worst. Or maybe it was just the expression behind it: that expression like she wouldn't mind seeing Nadine just disappear for being younger and prettier than her, and not knocked up yet.

Nadine once told her mother how she hated going to Mother Kralik. She thought she could confide in her mother, but she was wrong. Her mother slapped her a good one for shooting off her mouth, because Mother Kralik was her friend. Or, rather, Nadine's mother hung out with Mother Kralik just like all the other hags did, because they were too afraid not to.

Which is why Nadine never told her mother about what happened whenever she was sick. If she told her mother that, she would've been beaten for a week — for "lying," or "disrespecting an adult," or some shit like that. Mother Kralik stuck stuff in her. Like radishes and cigarettes — because this was part of "the healing process." Mother Kralik had told Nadine not to tell a soul, or the magic wouldn't work. And it wasn't so much that Nadine minded the process, but more so the humiliation, to be covered in sweat and trying not to puke, with that putrid tooth gleaming down at her and into her wide openness. It just wasn't comfortable being totally exposed for somebody other than her father.

At least her father never sneered at her like Mother Kralik did. He did his business, pulled out, shot his wad, and climbed off. And if he ever came inside her, at least it was only in her ass. Otherwise she would've had a little bastard. There was a severe lack of abortionists on the island.

"What are you looking at!" Mother Kralik suddenly demands.

Nadine looks up. "Nothing," she says and goes back to staring at her feet.

The next thing she knows, Mother Kralik has her by the neck. Nadine gasps and steps back, but the hull of the yacht blocks her retreat. Mother Kralik crushes up against her, breathing bacteria into her face.

Nadine tries to remain calm. This has happened before, and soon it will pass. All she has to do is give in, give up, agree, kiss ass.

"You're looking a little pale," Mother Kralik says, turning Nadine's head to the side and squinting at her skin. Out of the corner of her eye, Nadine can see a mustache coming closer.

"I haven't seen you for a while," Mother Kralik says. "What evil have you been up to?"

Nadine refuses to answer.

"Tell your mother to send you by," Mother Kralik snarls, then gives her a shove and turns away. But right when Nadine thinks she won't come back, Mother Kralik spins.

"Lemme tell you something," she sneers, lowering her brow and marching back, then pointing at something in her hand. "Sluts like this deserve what they got coming!"

Mother Kralik shows it to Nadine. It's a photograph in a fancy frame: a glamorous blonde in her mid-twenties, smiling, sexy, and strong. She is standing in front of the ship's wheel on the *Pacific Dream* proudly displaying a drink with a label reading SNAPPLE. She is wearing a captain's hat and a nipply T-shirt that says, I ♥ MY SHIP. Her boobs are enormous.

"Pacific Dream, bah!" Mother Kralik spits, picking a stuffed pink rabbit out of the sand and shaking it in Nadine's face. "Anyone with shit like this deserves to get their dream fucked up! Anyone with fluffy little foo-foo dreams about sailing around with champagne, waltzing in and out of other people's shitholes, just giggling away and wagging her ass around like a slut, well it's high time they learned that people get fucked! And dreams get fucked! Cuz there's no escaping getting fucked! Yep, it's the number-one law of physics. Shit gets squished!"

Mother Kralik hands the picture to Nadine and looks in her bag, listing what she's found: "Fancy perfume, cute little crystal thing, bath oil, shampoo, sassy little wristwatch, prissy little ruby ring, useless ivory elephant, brandy snifter . . . who needs this shit?!"

Nadine shrugs and looks at the picture. The hag speaks to the bag as if it were some bimbo: "You know what you are, honey? You're just a bag of shit like the rest of us! Yep, you're a walking, talking bag of shit! A mobile digestive system, baby, that's what you are! And you got squished! Your money and your sweet ass couldn't save you from that, now could it? Cuz that's the way it is! I mean, only a damn fool would think the world should be the way it isn't, cuz that's not gonna happen! Cuz that . . . that's fantasy-land, little miss princess! Little miss hoity-toity! Little miss Snapple-sipping bitch!"

Mother Kralik puts down her bag and starts in twisting her wrists. Nadine knows that Mother Kralik isn't talking to her, she's talking to herself — in a voice that's getting sharper and sharper.

"I hope you died out there!" Mother Kralik goes on. "Died screaming out there, little miss rich bitch! Little miss hot-to-trot, waving-your-tits-in-the-air, fat-free bitch! Little miss hot pants! I hope you died screaming and vomiting at the same time. Yeah, screaming and puking and drowning, salt water rushing in! Filling your lungs! Choking you, choking you . . . the ocean raping your precious little pussy! Your precious little perfumed pussy! Drying up your cunt! Shriveling you up! Turning you into one of us!"

Mother Kralik suddenly turns to Nadine, grabs the picture out of her hands, and snags a loogie on the glass. Then, just as quickly, she raises the picture above her head and smashes it on a rock, adding, "Sorry, Chuck!"

Who the hell Chuck is, though, Nadine doesn't know. She swallows hard as Mother Kralik stands there wheezing through her nose. Nadine doesn't say a thing. Both of them are looking down.

Then Mother Kralik kicks the sand and uncovers a half-buried gold-plated cross. It is highly ornate, about a foot long. Mother Kralik grabs it and thrusts it toward Nadine, holding it like a dagger.

"I've got my eye on you," she cackles, then gives Nadine a slap on the ass.

"Holy shit!" somebody suddenly yells. "Another shipwreck!"

Nadine looks up and sees some kid with an oversized Eric Clapton T-shirt standing on the rocks. Father O'Flugence is below him, with a purse on his shoulder.

"There's another one over here!" the kid yells again.

Immediately, the crowd drops what they're doing and makes for the rocks. Men crawl from the damaged bow, gripping bottles of wine. They take off after the women.

Nadine follows, running like a girl. When she gets to the rocks she starts to climb. One Eye is there to offer her a hand (on her ass), but Nadine leaps away before he can touch her.

When she gets to the top, her mother is there a couple levels lower. In fact, everyone is there, except the men scrambling up behind her. It is quiet. They are looking at a boat with winches and hooks, dashed on the rocks, dead black cod all over the place. Then Nadine sees the name: *The Jezebel.*

A horrified scream rises from the rocks. It's her mother. *The Jezebel* is her father's boat. And then she sees him, caught in a web of nets, bloated, half naked, and bound up like a ham. A gull is standing on his head, and he is missing an eyeball.

Nadine doesn't feel anything. She knows, however, that all eyes are turning her way, so she looks at her mother, who is clawing at her face. Grief is the socially correct response — but a bit too dramatic for what she feels, or doesn't feel. Nadine decides to wear a look of astonishment instead. She drops her jaw and stares at the man who used to force her into the pillow, backhand her so hard he'd split her lip, and call her a "no-good stinking twat!" Nadine exhales a sigh of relief, disguised as disbelief.

Below her, her mother is still screaming away, tearing at her eyes in agony. This is what they had both been hoping for but couldn't admit. A widow who doesn't wail is an insult to the island: it's the way they've been doing things ever since they can remember. It would be an insult to the town for her not to cry. So Nadine pretends to tremble at least, even though she's starting to realize she'll never have to smell his b.o. again. Or swallow his milky cum.

But more than that, she is glad for her mom, screaming away beneath her. The way her father shook her the night before he left — that will never happen again. And that stuff her father said to her — it'll never be said again.

"You fucking bitch! You fucking slut!" Nadine remembers her father yelling. "You've got the Devil in your cunt! In your old cow cunt! Out with the Devil!"

Her mother had begged like a wretch, repeating, "Please, please, please," over and over again.

"Fuck please!" her father had exploded. "Please fuck's more like it! You want it don'tchya?! You want it in your fat fucking cow cunt, don'tchya?! And so does your idiot daughter, the whore! You're both whores! Godless! Fucking! Sinning! Devil-whores! With Skanky! Stanky! Pussies!

Just dripping to get fucked! And suck cock! You cocksucking whores!"

Her father tossed his bottle across the room, and it shattered on the paneling. Usually he just passed out when he got this drunk, but this time he was in a rage, his face turning blue like a bruise.

"Now look what you've done, you fat! Fucking! Cocksucking! Whores! Get down on your knees and pray! Both of you, now! You filthy bitches! Pray for salvation! Repent! You fucking whores!"

Nadine didn't answer but got down on her knees next to her mother. She wished her dad would just molest her, and then they could all go to bed.

"Jesus . . . Oh Lord" — her mother's voice shook — "please, please forgive us . . . for . . . for . . ."

"For what, douche bag?!"

"For, for . . ."

Nadine remembers waiting for the blow. One of them was going to get it.

"For *what?!*" her father demanded again.

"For being what we are!" her mother finally burst out.

Nadine heard the sound of flesh on flesh and cried out because it wasn't her. She should've been the one getting hit, not her mother. She deserved it, not her mother. She was the whore, the bitch, the cunt, the reason for his anger . . .

Then something moves down in the boat. A plank falls over, and Yann comes stumbling out, covered with cuts and abrasions, a string of vomit streaming from his chin. There's a torn life jacket hanging on his shoulder.

"Praise God," Father O'Flugence exclaims. "It's Yann!"
"Fucking A right it is!" One Eye adds, standing next to him.

Nadine watches as Yann falls to his knees and barfs. Then barfs again and wipes his chin. She can tell he is oblivious to the fact that half the town is watching him, and she feels a sense of power in observing him in this state.

Yann is twenty-six, with shoulders and biceps that won't last long. He's a little pudgy around the waist, but among the men she's known all her life, he's the closest thing to Brad Pitt. Not that Nadine has ever seen a movie or a movie star, but she has seen *People* magazine.

Nadine watches as Yann goes through the dry heaves. She sees him turn around and look at the boat, and she sees the shock on his face when he discovers her father wrapped in the nets. She sees his jaw drop like hers had when she pretended to be upset at her father's death. Yann's expression, however, is genuine. He immediately presses his fists into his eyes, trying to smash the vision away.

Nadine starts to smile but catches herself. No doubt people are still watching her to see if she's a slutty little bitch or not. She goes back to her astonished expression, watching Yann but pretending her eyes are locked on her father.

Yann takes his hands away and looks at Nadine's father again; the gull is still pecking at his head. Yann picks up a shell and hurls it. The gull flies away, and Yann contracts into a ball. He grabs his knees and blubbers away, while Nadine, on the rocks, feels her nipples tingle. The best thing about him, she thinks, is he doesn't have a beard.

3

YANN TRIES TO MAKE SENSE of what just happened. He knows he's not too bright, but he figures he can figure it out. The thing is, his head can't recall whatever came first. Yann decides to relax and let his head unscramble itself.

He was at the Dirty Dawgfish . . . and everyone was smoking . . . except him. They were calling him a pussy for not smoking, but at least they couldn't call him nothing for not drinking. Everyone was drinking, especially the fishermen at the next table, burly fishermen, chugging whiskey as hard as they could . . . it was a drinking contest . . . there were at least fifty shot glasses lined up on the table and only five men. One guy threw a shot down his throat and blacked out. His chair fell over backwards, and his head hit the floor with a *thunk*.

Yann remembers the men standing over the guy and laughing at him. He remembers them whipping out their dicks and pissing on him. Everyone was laughing his ass off, but then . . . then a fight broke out. Who knows why? It just did, the way it always does when the air pressure's like it is because a front is coming in. He could feel it in his ears.

Someone broke a bottle, and the sound rang across the bar, followed by silence. Yann had to look. It was going to happen, and he could either look or not look. If he didn't look then he'd be a guy who didn't know how bloody it could be, and would therefore be a guy who could only imagine how bloody it could be, so he figured he might as well know the sight exactly rather than be a wuss about it.

This was different than not smoking or not shaving, or even playing the accordion. Yann knew he didn't have to be like them, with big fat guts and little mushroom dicks, fucking their kids and beating their wives. Yann had been to the movies. In Canada. He had seen other lives. Not everyone lived like people here, putting bullets through their heads. Like his father had done to his mother, and then to himself. He'd go away before that happened to him. He'd go away before he knocked someone up . . . then ended up like the men around him. He'd knock someone up somewhere else, then start his family there. His wife would be pretty and nice, and his kids would be innocent and protected. They would never see what he was about to see.

"Kill the fucker! Kill the fucker!" It was One Eye's voice. "Stab the sonuvabitch!"

Yann looked, knowing that what he was about to see would add to his impulse to get out. The bottle went up: sharp, jagged glass. The bottle came down. Right in the neck. The guy tried to scream, but his vocal cords were cut. All that came out were gurgles of blood.

What this has to do with the wreck, though, Yann doesn't know. But he knows that his head is clearing, and that he has landed on the island, and for this he owes something to God. He is alive and Bubba is dead. He doesn't even need to check on that. Bubba had died at sea, practically in his arms.

Yann looks over at Bubba again, and the vision makes him wretch. He opens his mouth to puke again, but nothing comes out except acids and salt. Closing his eyes, he sees the overcast. It's the washed-out sky from the day before.

They'd hit a good spot six miles out and had been laying longlines for cod. Or, rather, Yann was laying the lines while Bubba, up front, was getting drunk. And vicious. Yann figured Bubba hadn't gotten any action off his daughter. Too drunk to get it up most likely.

It was just the two of them. The rest of the crew, even One Eye, had refused to go out. Yann, however, was saving up. He needed all the money he could get. Crabbing down in Northern California was his goal, and he intended on making it happen. He'd get his own boat and live in the redwoods. He'd crab and fish and walk through the trees. He'd play his accordion and forget what he'd seen.

Yann dreamed on. For another couple hours he made plans like he always did when he fished with Bubba. And then they hauled up.

It was an incredible catch, with a big ugly cod every six feet, and sometimes a halibut. They were going crazy down there. But the pressure was getting lower and the foam was getting greener — and it wasn't a familiar green. Yann started getting ready to haul ass out of there.

"What the fuck you think you doing, dumbshit?!" Bubba demanded.

"Getting outta here," Yann answered, readying the crucifier, the machine that lays the longlines out, then hauls them back in, ripping the fish from the hooks. It was obvious: the darkness, the wind, the speed of the waves . . . a storm was coming. *The* storm was coming.

"Bait up!" Bubba ordered. "We'll leave if we see it, but right now we've hit pay dirt. We're gonna fill this motherfucker up and bring her back with more fish than a whorehouse down in Ketchikan! After this, you're gonna have pussy coming outta your asshole!"

Yann did what he was told. Bubba was the boss. He laid the longlines out again. And then he saw it, blacker than fuck and coming their way, from one end of the horizon to the other. But still, Bubba wouldn't give the order to haul up. In fact, he wouldn't even look at it. All he'd do was look at his almost empty fifth of whiskey.

Yann knew they were in for it. He fired up the winch and started hauling up. The crucifier whined, screeched, and came to a halt. Yann immediately cut the gas as Bubba came stumbling around the cabin, his face flushed with blood. "You fucking dumbshit!" Bubba roared. "Did I tell you to haul up?!"

"That doesn't matter now," Yann told him. "It's stuck."

Bubba looked at the crucifier's arc and the tautness of the line. They knew it was snagged, and they could feel the pressure coming closer.

"You fucking dumbshit!" Bubba yelled. "If we get caught in those fucking thunderheads, I'll fucking kill you! Fire them engines up!"

Now they'd have to back up and haul in the lines until they got to whatever they were snagged on, passed over it, and hopefully came free. It was either that or lose all that cable and tackle. Hundreds of dollars down the shitter.

Yann hit the ignition. Nothing. The battery was dead.

"You fucking idiot!" Bubba screamed. His face had gone from crimson to purple. He pulled out his gun and leveled it between Yann's eyes, but Yann just stared back. If Bubba put a bullet through his head, there'd be one less fisherman on their crummy little island. No big deal. Yann stared back.

Bubba's eyes were glassy and unsteady. He was sweating like a pig, his lips were quivering. The rain began to patter on the deck. Bubba cocked the hammer, muttered something, swung the barrel away from Yann, pulled the trigger, and the gun went off, blasting through the longline.

Then Bubba shot the other one just for dramatic effect. They could've brought that one in. Bubba turned around, and Yann was gone.

"Where the fuck are you!" Bubba bellowed and went stumbling toward the stern. Yann had pulled up the trapdoor covering the engine and climbed down in the hold. He was prying at the top of the battery with a screwdriver. It was a big marine battery, stolen from a Russian wreck. He got the top off.

"These cells are dry," Yann said, looking up at him.

Bubba put his gun away. "Get out of the way!" Bubba ordered.

Yann climbed out, and Bubba went down and unzipped his pants. He started taking a leak into the battery, slopping piss all over the place.

"Ain't there another battery onboard?" Yann asked.

"You think I got money coming outta my asshole?" Bubba barked. "Get up there and fire up the engine, dumbshit!"

And that's when the sheet rain hit. Bubba was still pissing when Yann hit the switch. There was too much water on the battery, in contact with both terminals. A bright yellow arc leapt up, followed Bubba's piss, and went right into his dick.

"*Fuck!*" Bubba yelled and lurched back, smacking his head on the door. He was instantly knocked out, so fell forward. His fat chest flopped on top of the battery, and his mass jerked gelatinously. His heart stopped, and the smell of burnt flesh rose from the hold.

Yann spun, saw this, and leapt from the controls. He pulled Bubba off the block and saw where the terminals had burned him a new pair of nipples. Bubba was dead.

The rain fell even harder. In the thirty seconds Yann held Bubba, they became totally soaked — while the battery, still exposed, began shorting out. Yann could feel the amps running through them both. Wherever there was water, there was current.

A popcorn sound started going off in the fuse box. Yann kicked the positive cable and ripped the clamp off. This didn't do much, but it really didn't matter. *The Jezebel* was a sitting duck.

Yann pulled Bubba out of the hold and closed the cover. He stepped back, then looked out to sea. It was enormous, rushing toward him, rising above him, almost upon him. A dead gull thunked against the hull. Then another. Yann could see hundreds of them, all around him. They were passing him, and the waves were getting choppier, reflecting the flashes blasting above.

"God save me," Yann said, making the sign of the cross on his chest. He strapped a life jacket on, found Bubba's bottle of whiskey, took a slug, then dropped to his knees and prayed to God, asking to get washed up on the island.

When the big waves hit, the starboard side was to the wind. Yann had just finished securing Bubba in some nets when a twenty-foot wave knocked the boat off balance, and a thirty-foot one lifted the keel right out of the ocean. Yann yelled, and the next wave broadsided the ship, flipping it over. He was thrown into the hold with the cod, all of them slamming and slapping against each other. He could feel the wave on top of the boat, forcing it down. Everything was black and crashing around him.

Yann opened his mouth to gulp some air but sucked in salt water instead. The next thing he knew, he didn't know nothing. The frigid blackness of the storm, the oily blackness of the hold, and the blackness in his head became one.

But now that blackness is gone, and Yann is thanking God. Not that he believes in God, but he's been trained to thank God, as if the Lord is some guy who saved his lily ass.

Looking up to the heavens, however, he sees something he never expected. It's Nadine, standing on the rocks above him, staring strangely down at him.

Last time Yann saw Nadine, it was in some nudie pictures Bubba had shown him. Yann had looked at those photographs for the same reason he had looked at the guy getting stabbed in the neck — which he also had trouble looking away from.

The wreck of the ship and the death of Bubba instantly disappear. Now, all he can see is Nadine, with a queer look in her eyes. Why is she looking at him like that?

Yann stares back at Nadine, up there with her tits and her ass that Bubba had shown him, and he feels sorry for her. She is no pathetic whore, she is just a kid. With something between her legs. Something he has seen.

Then Yann sees the rest of them, also staring down at him. Father O'Flugence is up there too. Even One Eye.

"Fucking A!" the voice of a child suddenly rings out. "There's another stiff over here!"

All heads turn toward the kid with the Clapton shirt. He's a little farther down the rocks, standing above a cave, pointing into it.

Yann immediately jumps up and tears his life jacket off. He doesn't even know he's climbing the rocks until he finds himself scrambling past the starfish and anemones. It isn't that he really cares who it is that got washed up, but he doesn't like being the center of attention, especially when he has just been in the fetal position, crying like a baby.

Yann tops the rock and looks where the kid is pointing.

What he sees stops him dead in his tracks. In the mouth of the cave, washed up on the sand, are a set of breasts so amazing, so exquisite, so magnificent, that Yann can hardly fathom them. Nothing like this has ever been seen on the island before.

4

VEN BEFORE YANN HEARS her heartbeat, he knows she is alive. He is also conscious that she is braless beneath her see-through shirt, and it is cold in the cave. He can feel her nipple against his cheek.

And then she moans, and her eyelids twitch. She moans again, and parts her lips. And the way they separate from each other, revealing the most pink-red of her tongue inside, immediately conjures other visions — which Yann, disgusted at himself, shakes from his head. This person is hurt, she needs help.

The town arrives behind Yann, pressing into the cavern to see the stunning stranger wearing nothing but a tight T-shirt and a pair of panties. There is silence. From twenty or thirty steps away, all the men and women stare. Since no one on the island has ever seen such mammaries before, they are dumbstruck. All of them.

Eventually, though, the kid who discovered her breaks the silence, yelling, "Hey, it's that bitch from *Baywatch!*"

"No it's not!" Yann says and stands up. He shoots the kid

a glance, which immediately shuts him up. Besides, nobody here even has a TV, since there's no reception on the island. If this kid knows about *Baywatch*, it's from *People* magazine.

Yann looks over at One Eye, surprised to see him so tranquil. A guy like him would be expected to shout out obscenities at a time like this, but he has a dreamy look on his face instead and is weirdly serene — as are all the men. Some of them even have their hats off.

"She's breathing," Yann tells the crowd. "She's just knocked out."

Then Yann sees Nadine again and quickly looks away. She'd been watching him a bit too closely. Before, her expression had intrigued him, but now it does the opposite. She is pissed at him — even though they don't know each other. Danger, Yann thinks.

Mother Kralik comes elbowing through the crowd, still wielding the crucifix. She sees the stranger on the sand and immediately jerks to a halt, shocked at the form lying before her with a sopping I ♥ MY SHIP emblazoned across her wet chest.

The vessel in her liver-spotted forehead instantly rushes with blood and swells to bursting proportions. "Well, well, well!" Mother Kralik snaps, loud enough for everyone to hear. "If it isn't that rich bitch from the ship!"

She spins and faces the faces she knows, which have always been too pale and meek to question her. She's yanked half of them from the womb and has earned her power over them by scaring them shitless during sickness. Some doctors use placebos; she uses fear — and it works.

Mother Kralik scans the islanders, then points the cross at the stranger. "Do you know what we have here? I'll tell you what it is! It's the Devil come up from hell to fuck with us!"

Eyes lower. People look down at the sand.

"Oh yes!" Mother Kralik goes on, her voice rising. "Lemme tell you, there's two types of rats in this shithole, people! There's the *whore,* and there's the *whorer.* And the *whorer* whores the *whore,* which is the *horror* of *whoring!* You're either a slut or a pimp in this shithole, either you're licking someone's ass or someone's licking yours!"

Yann turns away from Mother Kralik's ridiculous blather and kneels down to see if the stranger has suffered any neck or head injuries. She'll have to be moved, he figures.

Meanwhile, Mother Kralik keeps on ranting: *"Whores,* I tell you, get rotten crotch infections, but *whorers,* they get back rubs and body massages! *Whores,* they smear dogshit in their hair, but *whorers,* they get shampoos and fancy conditioners! What do you get? I'll tell you what you get! You get dogshit! Because all of you, you're all *whores!* But this bitch, she ain't got dogshit in her hair, oh no! She's the owner of that shmancy yacht. Oh yes! She sails around and wiggles her fanny, that's what she does! What she's got in her hair costs more than you make in a week, yanking guts and clobbering fish! Do you see what I'm saying? *Whores* get turds, but *whorers* . . . they get ice cream with sprinkles on top!"

Yann ignores Mother Kralik. Nadine, however, can't help but listen, as well as be a bit impressed. She knows Mother Kralik is full of shit, but she does have a couple of points.

"You!" Mother Kralik snaps and points the cross at the crowd. "You all sleep in shit! Like pigs! You sleep in shit! But this bitch, this rich bitch sleeps in silk! Oh yes, and when she wakes up, she's gonna want her nice, pretty, silk sheets back! And she's gonna want you to go back to sleeping in shit! Just think! Just think what you've got in your bags. She's gonna want it all back! She ain't dead like those Canadians last year! Or the rest of them who would've wanted their shit back too! But we took care of them, now didn't we?! And it was nothing! So are you gonna have the balls to tell her to go to hell when she comes knocking at your door? Are you?! This stuff is rightfully ours! It washed up on our shore, God gave it to us! God gave her to us! To do with her what we will!"

Some mumblings of agreement arise from the crowd, mostly from the older women.

Mother Kralik continues. "Look! She's practically dead. I'm not suggesting nothing, but you know how it is when you gotta flopping flounder on the slime line. There it is making a ruckus, it's in pain, it's suffering, it's gonna die anyway. That's why we got fish clubs! It's nothing, and you know it. It's nothing to just — *Whap!* And the thing is, she'd do the same to us if the situation were reversed, and you know it! The *whore* and the *whorer* are naturally opposed!"

Mother Kralik turns from the crowd and takes a step toward Yann and the stranger. Some hags from the crowd start moving forward, getting ready. Mother Kralik is their leader. This is their island, dammit! Majority rules!

Mother Kralik raises the cross above her head and speaks to it as if it's some two-bit tart: "So . . . you thought the world was your playground huh? But now you ain't so sure about that! Cuz maybe you found out that life isn't just skipping through the daisies with a sweet-smelling cunt, now is it? Cuz around here, we are all *whores*, honey! All of us! But you, you're the *whorer*, and you washed up on the wrong shore, baby! Sailing on in with your Visa cards and French perfumes! For what?! For fucking *what*?!"

Yann is aware that something is amiss. He looks up and sees the women advancing. Some of them are even picking up rocks. His eyes go wide.

"Well I'll tell you what for." Mother Kralik sneers. "To find out that the *whorer* gets fucked! Fucked in the head! Fucked dead! Finito! That's it! And it matters about as much as bonking some stupid flounder on the head! Come on, *whores*, it's time for *justice!*"

Yann can't believe it. Mother Kralik has actually rallied the hags, and now they're coming at him with rocks.

But does Yann get up and run? Nope. He throws himself across the stranger.

"God damn you!" Father O'Flugence suddenly declares, and Yann looks up, surprised to hear such words from the priest. Father O'Flugence has come between Yann and the mob. There's a purse hanging off his shoulder.

"God damn you all to hell," Father O'Flugence goes on, "if you go through with this! Have all of you lost your sanity?"

Mother Kralik stops in front of the priest. How easy it would be, she thinks, to knock the old fart down. She could use the cross. What a statement that would be! She grips it tighter and locks her eyes on the side of his head, right above the ear.

The old shrews wait to see it happen. Yann waits, Nadine waits, One Eye waits. Even Father O'Flugence waits, not even praying. And everybody knows the old guy doesn't have a chance. He's dead meat.

But then, out of nowhere, Nadine comes up behind Mother Kralik, grabs the cross out of her hand and throws it in the sand. Mother Kralik spins around to see who the fool with the death wish is and receives a slap to the side of the face that knocks her to the ground shrieking with a bloody nose.

"What are you gonna do?!" Nadine yells at the mob. "You're gonna attack Father O'Flugence, stone Yann to death, and kill someone you don't even know?! What the fuck kinda people are you?! You should be ashamed of yourselves! We got bodies to bury, we got a town to rebuild! You've all gone wacko!"

"Here, here!" One Eye puts in.

"Yeah," the kid with the Clapton shirt adds, "what sort of an example are you setting for the youth of America?"

"This isn't America, you little shit!" Mother Kralik spits, focusing her wrath on the most defenseless person in the crowd. He immediately retreats.

Nadine stands next to Father O'Flugence, feeling her knees begin to shake. The old women are lowering their rocks. For a while, the only sound in the cave is that of Mother Kralik wheezing.

Then: "You'll pay for this, you little shit-smear!" she tells Nadine, wiping the blood from a nostril. She gets up and looks at her pack of crones standing behind her like a bunch of dolts. They never should've stopped to think!

Mother Kralik picks up the crucifix, snags a bloody gob in the sand, and turns and walks away. The hags follow.

"Thank you, my child," Father O'Flugence says to Nadine. "That was very brave of you."

Nadine doesn't even hear him. Her heart is beating out of control. She has never stood up to anyone in her life. If she ever had, her father would've had her ass in a sling. It's evil for the young to defy the old. But maybe that's why she did it — to defy his hairy ass, which can't do jack shit now!

Nadine spins around to run to Yann. To throw her arms around him. She feels that she can do this now — that it would be appropriate. She protected him, she saved him! She has the right to cover him with kisses because of that look they shared when she was on the rocks and he was on the sand.

But Yann has something else in his arms: that stinking rich bitch! That rich bitch she should've let Mother Kralik smear to death!

"Take her up to the church," the old priest says, wiping his brow. "We'll see what we can do for her."

Yann leaves. Everybody leaves. And nobody says anything to Nadine.

She follows One Eye out of the cave, and he doesn't even try to cop a feel. This insults her even more. She looks out at the gray shitty sea and hates it even more than herself. That should've been her in Yann's arms!

But then she sees her mother on the rock, still staring down at *The Jezebel*. Nadine climbs up to her.

"Mother," she says, and rushes to her breast. She tries to hug her, but her mother jabs an elbow in her gut. Nadine coughs, unable to breathe. She can't comprehend why her mother would do such a thing. Doesn't she know that she's her kid?

"Mother!" Nadine cries. "What's wrong?"

Her mother says nothing and refuses even to look at her.

"Mother!" Nadine cries again. "Why won't you talk to me? Why won't you even look at me?"

Tears stream down Nadine's cheeks. She tries to get in front of her mother, to make her mother look at her — but every time she does, her mother looks in another direction, refusing to speak.

"Please, Mother," Nadine pleads, "please, please, please!"

Her mother gets up and walks away.

Nadine looks down at her father. One Eye is cutting the nets away, and a couple of men are hanging around, waiting to lug the body up the beach.

It's all my fault, Nadine thinks. She opens her mouth to scream, but just as she is about to let loose, it hits her that there is somebody else she can blame — and by God she will! And not only that, she will get that rich bitch! Oh yes, that rich bitch will pay. She'll pay with her slutty life!

5

FATHER O'FLUGENCE PRAYS for the people. This storm has been hard on the town, everyone is under stress. It's obscured the vision of his flock, as it has every year, and has added to their fear of each other. But he will forgive them, and work with them, and try to understand them — even though he knows the battle will be lost. Satan has landed on the island.

But not in the form that Mother Kralik claims. Father O'Flugence is certain that the Devil could never invade such a heavenly creature as the young woman sleeping peacefully before him.

He gets up from his chair and looks again at her driver's license, which he found in her purse — complete with wallet, credit cards, checkbook, cosmetics, flare gun, and a few thousand dollars in cash — of which he pinched only a couple hundred bucks: "April Berger, California, 26 years old. Height: 5' 9". Weight: 120 pounds. Organ donation: Yes." Father O'Flugence blesses her again.

She is still out cold, due to a concussion, but at least she's bandaged now, and clean, and warm in his home. And in the hands of Sister Erma, who watches over her, and prays for her when he's not there.

Sister Erma enters the room. "How is she, Father?" the squat nun asks.

"She's getting better," he answers, "mumbling more and more. Did they find the doctor?"

"Yes," Sister Erma replies. "He's dead."

Father O'Flugence closes his eyes and lowers his head. The tempest has taken its toll. Already today he has held three funerals, and now he has to give another for that womanizing, no-good drunk Bubba Murphy, bless his soul.

He shakes his head and opens his eyes. "God pity us," he tells the nun, and she nods back. They look at April, fast asleep beneath a painting of Mary Magdalene being raised by angels. April's blond hair is everywhere; she has perfect skin, long lashes, and a healthy bosom.

"Oh," the priest remembers, "any luck finding clothes?"

Sister Erma sighs and turns away with embarrassment. "No, Father," she says. "I've been asking around, but none of the women seem to be very enthusiastic about donating anything. I'll try again later this evening."

"Well," Father O'Flugence says, walking toward the door, "I'm sure something will turn up. But now I better go bury Mr. Murphy. Will you be all right?"

"Oh, I'll be just fine," she says, "don't you worry. I'll keep my eye on her. She seems to be doing all right. Poor thing, she's probably just exhausted."

Father O'Flugence forces a smile and closes the door softly behind him. He descends the stairs, puts on his coat, and leaves the house.

Outside, it is a whole different world. Despite the heavy drizzle soaking the dusk, chain saws can be heard droning throughout the town. Hammering can also be heard, and the shouts of men lifting things. The streets are full of sand, and trees are down everywhere. There are fish on people's roofs, and sea-soaked gulls on the lawns. Luckily, though, only a few people died. This year the destruction is mostly property. So far, that is.

Father O'Flugence walks around the church and enters the graveyard. What's left of the Murphy family is gathered in black: Nadine, Widow Murphy, and Bubba's two retarded sisters; Yann is also there — all of them standing beneath the tarp strung above the freshly dug grave.

Father O'Flugence is impressed that Yann showed up when no one else from *The Jezebel* cared enough to brave the rain. But still, he's not surprised that Yann is there. Father O'Flugence has always fancied Yann a decent, noble lad, and a handsome one at that.

Aye, the old priest thinks, he'd make a fine husband for Nadine . . .

Approaching the coffin, Father O'Flugence blesses Nadine once more in his head. All night long, and all morning too, he has been blessing this girl he thought would never amount to anything. What she had done in the cave was a godsend. He never knew she had such spine. To stand up to Mother Kralik was something even he couldn't do.

Nadine nods at the priest, who solemnly ducks under the tarp. She wonders if the old dust-farter knows she slammed the door in Sister Erma's face. The nerve of that old holy hole, coming around and asking for clothes for that rich bitch! Let her buy her own stinking clothes to cover her fat-ass tits with . . .

"Hello, Father," Nadine says respectfully.

"Hello, Nadine," he greets her, and then the other pallid faces. Widow Murphy does not nod back. The word is out that she has lost her mind, but Father O'Flugence knows it's just shock. A shock that's not uncommon on the island. She could emerge soon, or never at all.

"Please join hands," Father O'Flugence says. He sees Nadine blush but reach out for Yann. Yann, so it seems, is nervous, and looking a bit uncomfortable. His suit is too tight, and his tie is too short. Nadine finds his hand and grips it.

The six of them form a ring around Bubba's coffin, and Father O'Flugence starts in with the words he knows too well. He talks about what an outstanding citizen Bubba was, how he loved his daughter, his wife, and his crew, and how he will be missed by all. Secretly, however, he observes the mourners.

Widow Murphy is staring straight ahead, with a look on her face like nobody's home. As for the retarded sisters, it's amazing that they can even stand up, their expressions being exactly the same. Yann, by contrast, appears sincerely downcast. And then there's Nadine, clenching his hand so tightly that her knuckles have turned white. She keeps looking at Yann but hardly ever at the casket.

Then, after Father O'Flugence says everything, he signals the driver of the van, who brought Bubba's sisters from the home on the other side of the island. He comes and helps Yann lower the coffin into the pit, then he takes the sisters away.

Yann, however, stays to help Nadine and Father O'Flugence fill in the grave. Nadine's mother just stands there watching. After a while, flowers are laid on the mound.

"God bless you," Father O'Flugence tells Nadine, repeating what he can't stop repeating. It's the popular phrase of the day, thanks to the storm. Empty embraces are exchanged, and then the priest walks off, escorting Widow Murphy home.

Now Nadine and Yann are alone. She looks up at Yann, and Yann looks down at her. What she sees is one hunk of a man, bound by clothes, wet with sweat and rain. She'd like to stroke his head. He could suckle her and she could stare into the distance with a supplicating look on her face.

What Yann sees, however, is a pathetic, homely girl who's been deceived by her father, and he pities her. She has no clue that he has seen her naked. She doesn't even know that what she has is what he sees when he wakes up with a woodie: that jet black patch, that fleshy ass, those pert little tits — man, what he would give to give them a lick!

"Nadine," he asks, "why'd you do that in the cave?"

"Because," she says, "they were gonna kick your ass, Yann."

Yann and Nadine stand there for a while and listen to the rain. It is much darker than before. The silence hangs in the air like a parlor-room fart, both of them pretending it doesn't exist.

"Thanks," Yann eventually says.

"Sure," she answers back.

They are both staring at the mound of dirt that used to be her father. Then, after a while, Yann speaks again. "I just wanted to tell you," he says, "your dad was a . . . a . . . a swell —"

"Cut the shit, Yann," Nadine suddenly tells him, spinning on one foot and glaring up and into his eyes.

Yann gulps. The look she's giving him makes him want to piss. "I think I gotta go take a leak," he tells her. "I mean, umm . . . "

She grabs him, pulls his head down, and jams her tongue inside his mouth. Yann can tell their lips don't fit. Between them, there is no magic whatsoever. What he feels is absolutely nothing. But still, he kisses back as Nadine makes out even harder, stabbing her tongue around in a frenzy and digging her nails into his neck.

"Owww!" Yann yells and pulls back. "That hurts."

"Oh!" Nadine exclaims. "I love you too!"

Yann pretends he didn't hear what he just heard. This chick is delusional and he knows it. But still . . . he could get a piece. And then they could break up.

Yann grabs Nadine and pulls her against him. They make out some more, his boner between them like an iron rod.

"Are you hungry?" she finally asks, pulling back.

"Yes," he says, faking a saintly, dewy expression.

She takes his hand, and they walk down the hill together. He is hard and she is wet. Lightning flashes in the sky.

6

A PRIL WAKES UP and stares through the room. This is not her place in L.A., this is somewhere else. There are shepherd scenes on the wall, and pictures of Jesus, Mary, Moses, the whole gang. Whose bed was she sleeping in now?

The last thing she remembers is sailing out of Dutch Harbor. She was taking the producer of her next movie, Karl Ronson, up to see the ice floes. It was a corporate deal. He got to watch her tits and ass, and she was allowed to write it off. She didn't like sleeping with the creep, but that was what she had to do to get the deal. Once the director signed on with Ronson, she'd be in for a seven-figure paycheck, but first she had to spread her legs. That's show business.

Anyway, it wasn't all that bad. The guy got so drunk he could hardly get it up, the food was good, and the scenery was superb. She'd be back in a week and on the set, and Ronson would be somewhere else, getting sucked off by some Hollywood whore.

She, however, was not a whore! She was a damn hard

worker, who other workers — her agent, the director, a whole cast of actors, technicians, stuntmen, even the pimply key grip — depended on. And if she didn't giggle and wiggle and jerk Ronson off, they'd all end up shooting porno — which was why she was chauffeuring him around in her private yacht and letting him lick her award-winning tits. For the team.

But where the hell was she now? April places a hand on her forehead and feels a bandage. Pressing on the bump beneath it, she winces. She hasn't had a crack on the head like that since she was thirteen and learning to sail. The boom had swung in and knocked her off the deck. When they pulled her out, she was bleeding pretty bad, but still was conscious enough to tell her father she'd get that boom back.

And since then she had, by conquering the winds. Not only had she sailed around the world by herself but she had sailed right into Hollywood, where she starred on a popular television show, then became a movie star. Or, rather, a multimillion-dollar corporation with big tits.

April remembers sailing north of Nome, but that's about it. It started getting cold. Something was interfering with the weather channel. She was looking at the maps — that was it! Going through the Bering Strait, she figured she could ride the shoreline or cut straight up and avoid the traffic of tankers, so that was what she did. The wind was blowing good. She figured it would get them up there pretty quick. And the sooner the trip was over, the sooner she could start forgetting Ronson grunting from behind. What a loser! He could hardly get it in half the time.

After he had his way with her that night, though, and

she pretended she liked it, April decided to sail until dawn. They'd get there in the morning, he'd take his pictures, she'd pretend she wasn't exhausted, and then they'd turn around and head back. So she put on a T-shirt, some bikini bottoms, and a parka over that, and flicked on the running lights, sailing into the wind.

April loved sailing at night, but this was not Tahiti. Setting her bead on the North Star, she switched the radio on, but all she got was static. Eventually, though, she picked up a signal. It was old-fashioned Morse code: three long beeps followed by three short beeps, repeating over and over again. No doubt some kid messing around. She turned the radio off.

Near dawn and past Cape Hope she started getting tired. Her ears were playing tricks on her. There was a rumbling, but still nothing obscured the stars. And it couldn't have been thunder, because the sky was clear as far as she could see.

Then she heard a slight thump against the bow, and then another. April turned the spotlight on. She was cutting through a current of birds. Dead birds. Seagulls. Hundreds of them. She shined the spotlight into the wind.

And that was when she discovered that what she thought was the horizon was not the horizon — it was actually something over the horizon, along the horizon, and as black as the sea. And it was growing, and rising above her, and humming. Then she saw a flash, and felt the rain. She was sailing straight into it.

Three seconds later April was hit by hail. She was so surprised that she let out a squeal. A chunk hit her like a fist in the mouth. She couldn't believe it. Another one hit a

porthole behind her and shattered the glass. The sails began to slap and snap. She had to come about.

April ducked and spun the wheel. Ever bigger hail
rained down on her back, pelting the parka. She'd have to
get inside and sail from there. Another chunk hit her in the
head. She screamed.

"What's going on up here?" Ronson asked, opening the
door and sticking up his head. The boom swung down and
hit him in the skull. April heard the crush of bone as he
flew right out of his slippers and was flung into the sea.
The rope caught, the sail filled, the jib expanded, and the
boat took off wing-in-wing.

April screamed again — but what could she do? She
couldn't turn the boat back into the eye of the wind, clip-
ping along at thirty or forty knots. Besides, Ronson was already a quarter mile behind with a smashed-in head,
bobbing in her freezing wake. She'd never find him.

Blam! Thunder blasted right behind her. The hail had
stopped, but the rain was just as furious. April looked over
her shoulder, and it hit her in the face like bird shot. Nevertheless, she covered her eyes and peered into the storm.
There was a line of foam hovering above her. It was the
crest of an enormous wave bearing down on her. She didn't
even have time to don a life jacket. The wave lifted the
stern into the air, and the boat went vertical as she leapt
into the icy waters. The next thing she knew, her parka was
pulling her down and she was struggling to unzip it. That
was all she remembered.

"I'm alive," she hears herself say.

"Thank God indeed," a kindly voice replies.

April looks toward the door opening before her. A priest is there bearing flowers.

"These are from some admirers," Father O'Flugence says — and she immediately directs him to put them by the window. It's a reflex reaction.

"I knew you'd come to," he tells her, smiling like a pervert. At least that's what April thinks at first. Never trust a priest — that was her motto. They don't just go for little boys . . .

"Where am I?" she finds herself demanding, surprised at the snotty tone in her voice. "Alaska?"

"Well," the priest says, "I guess you could say that. Your ship was caught in the storm. You washed up on an island in the middle of nowhere. This is my home . . . my name is Father O'Flugence."

"Well," April says, "did you find any other bodies?"

"A man in pajamas?"

"Yes, that's him."

Father O'Flugence pauses, then answers slowly. "Yes, I heard he was found, but not in very good shape."

April's voice is shaky. "He was dead. I saw the boom hit him in the head."

Father O'Flugence looks at the floor. He speaks softly, lying: "His remains have been buried."

Both of them are silent for a while. Then April speaks up. "I need to make some phone calls."

"Yes," he says, "but I want to send Sister Erma by to check on you first. She used to be a nurse."

April nods, just to get the old guy out of her room.

"I'll be back with some crumpets," he tells her and turns toward the door.

Crumpets, April thinks, what the hell is this place?

Father O'Flugence leaves, and April immediately throws off the covers to see what she's wearing. It's a blasé floral smock. If that asshole touched her . . .

April sits up and tries her limbs. Everything still works. How she survived in that water, she'll never know. She wonders if she experienced any brain damage, then stands up, feeling weak but strong enough to go to the flowers. No card. Typical. April looks out the window.

Outside, a quaint little town is coming alive. People are out and working in their yards. Simple folk, with simple clothes and simple tools. Grandmas, Grandpas, bearded men. And cats! There are cats all over the place: lazing in the morning sun, licking paws, climbing trees, rolling in the grass.

April always wanted a cat but had always been so busy jet-setting that if she'd ever got one, she'd have had to leave it with her mother — and then the cat would have become her mother's, not hers.

She opens the window. "Hi, cats," April sings to them, "hi there, hello, yoo-hoo."

An old man and an old woman look up from collecting sticks. The old woman immediately looks away, but the old man stands transfixed. To April, this is not uncommon. He probably saw her on *Baywatch*.

Two knocks sound on the door. "Come in," April says, jumping back into bed. A nun walks in, smiling like an idiot, holding a bundle of something.

"I see you're looking better, dear," Sister Erma says, and approaches. "How do you feel?"

"Great," April says, faking it.

Sister Erma peers in April's eyes, then asks her to stick out her tongue. She does it.

"You look fine to me," Sister Erma says. "I wish we could send our doctor up, but he's in heaven now."

"I'm sorry," April lies.

"Well," the nun says, placing the bundle on the bed, "I have some clothes here for you. I apologize that they aren't what's in fashion these days; there is a very uncharitable streak on the island at the moment. But you must understand, the storm wreaked havoc upon us all, and it takes a while to recover."

April unwraps the bundle. It's a nun's outfit.

"It belonged to Sister Stephanie. I think it will fit you," Sister Erma says. "She's in heaven too."

"No hat?" April laughs, pretending to have heard Sister Erma. The idea of dressing up in nun duds is pretty hilarious to her. Only in Hollywood . . .

Sister Erma is aghast that April would laugh at Sister Stephanie's death. However, she realizes that the poor little lamb has lost her way and, like the people of the town, is no doubt under stress.

"Your undergarments are over on the dresser," Sister Erma says. "I had them washed, but I'm still looking for more clothes for you. You're welcome to wear these until we find more. Maybe a ship will bring something in."

"Thank you, Sister," April says, "I really appreciate it."

Sister Erma goes out, and April automatically reaches for a remote control. It takes her a few seconds to realize there isn't a TV in her room. Not even a phone.

7

AFTER CRUMPETS, April goes out, the sexiest nun in town. She swivels her hips and breathes in the fresh fish air. This place is just too much, she thinks, and nods at people on her walk. She is ecstatic to be alive.

Down at the docks, she looks for a pay phone. They didn't even have one at that backwards-ass country church. She finally locates one — but hesitates. What's she going to do? Call up her mother and tell her she's all right? Yes. And then what? Call up Larry, her agent, and tell him that Ronson is dead? Call the police? Call *Entertainment Tonight?* Go back to Hollywood and strut her stuff? Suck cock? Take it in the ass?

"Fuck that!" April says and decides to wait a bit. She's a millionaire, she can do whatever she pleases — and what she wants to do is check out this town where chance has landed her.

April walks out on the dock. Men are loading and unloading nets. A one-eyed fisherman smiles like an angel at her, and she nods back. All the men are gentlemen, eyes wide, jaws agape. No doubt they've never seen a forty-two-inch bust in a nun dress before, except of the old fat saggy variety.

But anyway, the politeness is enchanting. They take off their hats and gaze into her eyes, greeting her with "Mornin' ma'am" and "Nice day, eh?" And no flashbulbs go off in her face. And no lipstick mouths shove microphones at her. And no one wants an autograph. She's free!

April sighs and walks to the end of the dock, where a kid is playing with a kitten. He's wearing a Clapton T-shirt that's too big for him.

"Hello, kitty." April addresses the cat. It's a small yellow kitten with white paws, almost too young to be on its own.

The kid spins around with a genuine grin affixed to his face. "Hey, ain't you that lady?"

"What lady is that?" April asks, kneeling down to pet the cat.

"That washed up on the beach," the kid says.

"Yes" — April laughs — "I suppose that would be me."

"You a nun?" the kid asks, squinting.

"I guess I am," April says, "at the moment."

They both regard the cat, batting at its tail.

"My mom says I gotta get rid of it," the kid says. "Its mom died in the storm."

"There seems to be a lot of that going around." April smiles.

"Yeah," the kid says.

April picks up the cat. It nuzzles a breast and starts to purr.

"But what will you do with it?" she asks.

"I dunno . . . ice it."

"Oh . . . you're kidding."

The kid shrugs.

"I'll take this kitty," April tells him.

"Gee lady, like, thanks!"

April stands up and walks away with her new cat, holding it against her chest. She talks to it as she walks: "Hi, kitty . . . you're a cute little kitty. Oh yes you are."

At the end of the dock, April turns and walks toward the market. "You're a good kitty, oh yes. Good kitty, good kitty. Now you're my kitty, yes you are."

She walks by Mother Kralik, who is smoking cigs with a couple deformed sea hags. April doesn't even look up, just keeps going, tickling the kitten. Mother Kralik scowls and mutters something.

April keeps talking to the cat. "Do you like it here, kitty? I like it here. It's so laid-back . . . so relaxed. And beautiful. Who needs L.A.? Who needs it? Do you want to stay here, kitty? Huh, do you? I bet you do."

The old women watch as April disappears into the distance, swishing her ass like a floozy. The fishermen, though, watch her with reverence. A goddess is among them.

Then Nadine appears, coming down the hill, leading her catatonic mother. They are walking toward the market, and Nadine is trying to talk to her mother. But her mother still won't answer her.

Somewhere in the harbor, a foghorn blows. The smell of rotten fish floats up from the sand, rank enough to make a hound dog gag. April, however, is upwind of the smell.

8

SMOKING CIGS and chewing tobacco, the women stand in front of the junk store known as Mother Kralik's Antiques, which is closed for the season. It is late in the morning on a Saturday in early April, and the air is warmed by a renegade jet stream, which is not un-common on the island.

"Look," the old crone tells them, "if something doesn't happen soon, it'll be our ass! She'll bring in the feds, the world will know what we've done. I say we better do her like we did him, like we did all of them!"

Grunts of approval are vented from the women. Hairy moles and plaque-ridden teeth nod in agreement.

Mother Kralik is referring to the half-eaten man they found on the beach wearing pajamas. The sand-fleas had gotten him, but still, he had a wristwatch on, and a whole bunch of rings — which the hags knew would be worth a pretty penny to the Russians. So they cut the fingers off and removed the Rolex. Then did with him what they did to the Canadians the year before, and almost everyone that's ever washed up on their sand, compliments of God.

So far, it had worked pretty well. It didn't really matter what went into the mix, because the grinder ground it all into an indistinguishable mush. Shark, doll porpoise, cod — the Japanese didn't give a rat's ass. They were under contract, so came for their dog food every month.

"Did you see the way she was poo-pooing that cat?!" a semiretarded fishwife asks. "She must think her shit don't stink."

"That's right!" Mother Kralik agrees. "And did you see the way all the men pretended to be perfect gentlemen? Makes me sick!"

"Precious little cunt!" another hag puts in.

"Pretty little pussy!" another one scoffs.

Then Nadine comes walking up, leading her mother. They walk toward the women and stop. Nadine has a smarmy grin on her face — like she just got laid or something.

"Well, well, well," Mother Kralik says, picking at the blood clot in her nose, "if it isn't the little bitch who struck me the other day. Have you come to beg my forgiveness?"

"Oh," Nadine cockily says, "I forgot all about that."

Mother Kralik sneers and holds down the rising tirade in her throat.

"Okay, Maw," Nadine says, "here you are. I'll be back for you in a bit."

Nadine leaves her mother with her companions and walks off humming. She is heading to the market.

"Want a cig?" Mother Kralik asks Widow Murphy.

Widow Murphy nods. It's the first acknowledgment she's given anyone, of having heard anything anyone's said, since her husband died. Mother Kralik places the cig between her lips and lights it for her. They all watch Nadine go into the market.

"Little whore," Mother Kralik says, "she sure has copped an attitude. She's got something coming!"

All the women nod and spit.

Nadine walks past bins of crabs, oysters, and illegal salmon. She stops at the sea cucumbers and smiles two rows of almost straight teeth. Reaching into the bin, she removes the largest, squishiest one, and fondles it.

Yeah, she thinks, she can still feel the cum dripping down her leg.

Actually, though, it isn't semen, it's her own excitement, because she's still horny and generating juices. Already, Nadine believes she is preggy.

After the funeral, they had gone back to her trailer, where Nadine started cooking dinner and her mother and Yann just sat there. She was making macaroni and cheese. As they waited for the water to boil, she excused herself, went into the bedroom, and slopped on way too much makeup. When she came out the water was boiling. She saw how Yann noticed her transformation and mistook the shock on his face for her dazzling effect. Dinner was served.

"Have some macaroni and cheese," Nadine said to her mother, shoving the bowl across the table. But her mother just glared at her, and then at Yann. They all sat there for an awkward three minutes, no one saying anything. Then her mother took her hand and stuck it right into the macaroni and cheese. Like a monkey flinging shit, she grabbed a handful and threw it right in Nadine's face, staining much of her makeup with orange food coloring.

Again, the three of them sat there, not saying anything. Eventually, though, her mother got up, went into her bedroom, and slammed the door behind her. Both Yann and Nadine breathed a sigh of relief.

"Gosh," Yann said, reaching over to pick some noodles off her shoulder, "that was, umm . . . intense."

Nadine looked like she was about to cry. She didn't even try to wipe the sauce off her face. Yann, however, took his napkin and started cleaning her off. Every time he went for a drip, he'd remove a layer of skin-colored base.

"Maybe I just oughta go," he told her nervously.

"No," she said, and made him stay in his seat, holding him there with her eyes. Yann tried to make conversation.

"So . . . ummm . . . when's the last time she spoke?"

"Day he died."

"Maybe that was a bad question."

"No, it wasn't," Nadine told him, "it was real."

"Some questions are better off left unasked," he said. The conversation was going pretty good.

"If it's there," Nadine said, "why pretend it's not? It's dumb to pretend that something there ain't there if it's there."

"Huh?"

Nadine didn't answer. She lit up a cig and blew out a big plume of smoke. They watched it linger in the air. Neither of them felt much like eating.

"Okay," Yann finally said, "if something's there, and it's real, and it's dumb to pretend it's not there . . . then maybe we should talk about what you're thinking . . . and what I'm thinking . . . cuz, I mean, let's face it, ummm . . ."

"Keep going, Yann."

"Like . . . it's there, which is why we're here, cuz, you know . . . do you know what I'm saying?"

Nadine blew a smoke ring out, and it floated toward his face. "Say it, Yann."

"Why me? Why not you?"

"Okay," Nadine said. "Fuckin'! That's what we're talking about, ain't it? Fuckin'!"

Yann suddenly felt sick. He didn't want to be talking to her about this. There were plenty of other dark triangles. The way she put it made it seem so crude, even though that was why he was there — because he was afraid of going to a whore. He shoved his macaroni away.

"Ain't it?" Nadine pressed on. "Ain't that why you're here? Or are you really hungry?"

"I'm not hungry anymore."

Nadine felt Yann slipping away. He was looking everywhere in the room other than in her direction. She saw him swallow hard. She had to act fast.

Standing up, she shoved the table over. Macaroni and cheese, dishes, glasses, and silverware went crashing to the floor. Yann looked up at her with a combination of astonishment and fear. Was she going psycho?

Now there was no table between them. Nadine took a step toward him, then suddenly sat down on his lap, facing him.

"Uhh . . . I don't know about this," Yann said.

"Shut the fuck up, Yann," she said, yanking his head back. She went to town licking his neck, thinking this would turn him on. But in his pants, his dick was shriveling up.

Nadine moved forward, positioning her big wet muff right on top of his crotch. She wasn't wearing any underwear. Nadine never wore underwear. All underwear ever did for her was collect skid marks.

Her pussy began to squish around. She started thrusting it up and down, all the while cramming his head into her breasts. Yann started making some sort of feeble attempt at biting at her nipples through her dress. Then she felt his hands on her ass — her bare ass. Yann had ventured under her skirt and was gripping a butt cheek in each hand.

It felt like forever, grinding against him, until he finally got an erection. The moment he touched her asshole, though, she felt his dick leap beneath her. Nadine started rubbing harder, as Yann poised a finger on her sphincter.

"Oh, Yann," she cried, "I want you to fuck me so hard you rip my cunt wide open."

Yann's dick started to get soft.

"Don't talk," he told her and slipped his finger in a bit. Why he was doing this, she didn't know. Maybe he was a fudge man. But she acted like she liked it, and after a few more minutes of grinding against him, she actually did. She thought about telling him to shove his finger even farther up her poop-chute but decided not to. Maybe her voice would remind him who he was with, and then he'd lose his boner, which was now a full and furious hard-on.

Nadine felt her anus tingle. She felt like she had to take a crap but kept on thrusting anyway. Yann had worked a tit out of her blouse and had practically the whole thing in his mouth. She reached down and unzipped his pants, and his cock sprang out, long and curvy, throbbing healthy — not pale and dinky like her father's. Nadine gasped. She had to have it inside her.

All it took was a lift of her hip. When she brought it back down, Yann's cock was way up inside her, touching a part of her that even her finger couldn't reach. The only thing that had ever gone that far inside her before was a Coke bottle inserted by Mother Kralik. And Yann's cock, of course, felt a whole lot better than that. She felt something like melty butter oozing through her. Immediately, her loins began to quiver.

Yann took his finger out of her bunghole and grasped both buttocks in his hands. He started raising and lowering her, but she needed it faster. A couple seconds later she was bouncing up and down on his dick. Every time she descended, he'd spank her buns back into the air. Things were rushing hot within her. Nadine felt her skin go clammy. She was about to come for the first time in her life without jerking off.

Yann pulled out and shot his wad. Nadine opened her eyes and saw him leaning back and slowing down. The whole ordeal only lasted thirty seconds. Her vision blazed white-hot — the fucker! She grabbed his wet cock and tried to jam it back inside.

"No," Yann said, suddenly opening his eyes, "it's got jizz on it. You might get —"

"So what?!" Nadine snapped, and Yann immediately went limp. Nevertheless, she tried to get it back in. She weaseled in the head, but Yann wouldn't have it. He tossed her off his lap, stood up, zipped up, grabbed his coat, and ran into the rain. The door banged behind him.

Spread-eagle on the linoleum, her skirt hitched up, Nadine looked at the fluorescent light flickering above and stared at it until all she saw was one vast burst of purple. She placed her hand on her stomach, felt a jab of gas, and imagined it was a tiny kick. Then she smiled a dreamy smile that lasted all night and into the following day.

"Until we meet again, my handsome stud," she said to the all-consuming purpleness. "You fucked me good, you fucked me good . . ."

9

WEARING JEANS and an oversized sweatshirt, April answers the door of her cute new house, which she bought the day before yesterday on a whim. Since there wasn't a hotel on the island, and the idea of living with Father O'Flugence didn't really turn her crank, she just up and bought the place from some widow who didn't have any business sense at all. So now she and Poo-poo have a new home.

On her porch, April sees a vision from the past. It's Widow O'Reilly and Widow Flanahan, looking like pre–World War II bag ladies, squat and gray, with scarves around their lumpy heads. They are toting overstuffed bags.

"Oh do come in," April cheerfully invites them and steps back. They enter, waddling into the center of the empty room, where they plop down their bags and immediately start rummaging through them. April helps herself to one of their sacks.

"Maybe this will fit," she says, holding up a flowered

dress, then setting it aside. She picks out a couple shirts. Most of the clothes are dingy and gray. Tan and blue are a rarity. Widow O'Reilly shows her a couple of skirts.

"Don't you have anything in happier colors?" April asks, and the widows give each other an exasperated look. They pick through the clothes for a while.

"Okay," April says. "I'll take this, and this, and this, and this. How much do you want for them?"

The widows just shrug.

"Okay," April says. "In the United States, I mean in California, I'd probably pay a couple bucks for each of these in a thrift store, so how about" — she regards the toothless, wrinkled visages before her and suddenly feels generous — "oh heck, I'll give you twenty dollars for everything. I guess I'll be needing some rags anyway."

April goes to her purse, takes out a couple tens, and returns to the women. She gives them each a bill, but neither of them responds — they just pocket the money.

"Do you think you can find any shoes?" April asks. "And kitchenware?"

Widow Flanahan nods.

April walks them to the door, thanks them, and lets them out. She rolls her eyeballs at the sky, then closes the door. Such people!

Her kitten comes sliding across the floor, chasing a rubber ball. April bends to pick it up, but it scampers away, spinning its paws on the varnish. She laughs, then goes to the phone and dials.

"Hi, Mother," she says into the receiver. "No, I'm in Alaska. Guess what? I'm in love."

April listens to her mother for a bit and rolls her eyeballs once again.

"No, Mother, it's not a man this time, it's a place. I've fallen in love with a place. You should see it, it's so quaint. A little village on a little island. You should come and visit sometime, I'm sure you'll love it. But you'll have to bring cash, they don't accept credit cards here."

April listens for a minute.

"No, Mother, I'm not moving here . . . I *have* moved here. Property is cheap, I bought a place. A lovely little summer home, hardwood floors, front porch, gingerbread trim . . . it was a steal!"

April looks out the window and hears the response she expected. Her mother can't believe it. What about her career? What will she do there?

"Look, Mom, I don't know. The way I see it, it's like fate. I was getting sick of all that glamour, all those cameras, everyone wanting something from me. Who needs it? Screw it! I want to do something different. I want to live an ordinary life . . . like you. Like the people around me. I don't know, maybe I'll write a book or something. I've always wanted to be a writer. Oh, did I tell you, I got a lovely little kitten. Its name is Poo-poo."

While April's mother has a cow, she looks out the window and sees an old man in his yard, chopping at a stump with an ax. He stops, scratches his head, and bends his back. When he sees April standing in the window, she waves to him and he waves back. Then he goes back to work with renewed vigor.

"No, Mother, I don't have e-mail. I don't want e-mail.

And please, don't tell people where I am. I'd like some peace and quiet for a bit, if you please. And don't tell Larry Rubenstein yet, I'll call him at my leisure. What? He's there right now?"

April suddenly finds herself talking to her agent.

"Hey, Larry, what's up? Look, don't tell Mom because she'll totally flip, but Karl Ronson is dead. Yeah, we got hit by a storm and . . . huh? Okay, call me back on your cellular then."

April gives him the number and hangs up. She could feel Larry starting to go ballistic. Without her, he'd only have the Olsen twins. Larry is about to have a shitfit.

"Poo-poo!" April calls, but the phone immediately rings. Larry's on I-5, driving back to L.A.

"Listen, babe," he tells her, "you can't just call me from Alaska and tell me this! You can't just tell me that a millionaire and a billionaire go off and the billionaire dies and the millionaire isn't coming back! Have you lost your mind?!"

"First of all," April tells him, "stop calling me babe, I'm not your babe. And second of all, don't you raise your voice to me. I don't need you, Larry, I don't need Hollywood. Everyone wants a piece of my ass and I'm all out of ass, okay? Find yourself a new piece of ass to peddle."

"But, April," he says, "the world wants to know. The director's on my ass, Ronson's agency is on my ass, everybody's looking for you! They need you, *we* need you! You can't just say a guy like Ronson is dead with as little explanation as that! Do the police know?

"There are no police here."

"Great . . . Just great! Look —"

"No!" April tells him, "you look, I've made up my mind —"

"You're under contract!"

"*You're* under contract!"

"I'll sue!"

"I'll countersue!"

"I'll counter-countersue!"

"You will not; I know you, Larry."

"Well, just because I'm a friend of the family doesn't mean I won't be forced to sue. I mean, they're gonna sue me. And not only that, they're gonna ask me where you are and I'm gonna have to tell them. And I'm also gonna have to tell them that you said Ronson's dead. And then they're gonna come looking for you, they're gonna have all sorts of questions."

"Let them."

"Babe, I mean April . . . April, April, April . . . look, let's talk this out . . ."

"Larry," April tells him, "there's no talking. I've started a new life. I'm a writer now."

"You're a what?"

"You heard me."

"But, April —"

"I'll talk to you later, Larry. I'll be needing you to wire me money periodically."

She hangs up and rolls her eyeballs once again. Agents!

April tries to catch Poo-poo but can't. She decides to go for a walk. She picks up her purse and flounces out the door.

Outside, April admires her new house. "You're so cute," she tells it, "with your widdle picket fence and your widdle yard."

April cocks her head and looks at the yard. Her garden will need work. It's early in the spring, but warm enough to plant flowers. And maybe that kid with the Clapton shirt could mow her lawn.

April starts down the street, passing the other summer homes, all of which are abandoned at the moment. She swings her arms at her sides and bounces along. She passes Father O'Flugence heading up the hill and waves to him. He waves back, appearing a bit self-absorbed.

He's probably thinking about the money he pinched from her purse, April thinks, though she really doesn't give a damn about a couple hundred dollars. There were also some other things missing, but she didn't feel like making a fuss. After all, he did put her up.

April walks on and passes One Eye, who takes off his hat and bows with chivalry. She laughs at that and notices the solid young buck at his side — a good-looking kid who'd give Brad Pitt a run for his money. He smiles at her, and she smiles back, increasing the wiggle in her walk.

She comes to the only shop on the island, Mother Kralik's Antiques. It's not open yet, but she peers through the window. Inside, she sees a bunch of worthless junk: model ships, weather vanes, cuckoo clocks, et cetera. And then she sees something that belongs to her: it's her grandmother's golden cross, brought over from Heidelberg circa World War I, which her grandmother gave her for good luck and she had kept on the ship. But now it's in this store with a price tag on it of a hundred bucks. Shit, April thinks, it's worth at least a thousand in gold alone.

April goes to the door and turns the knob, but the store is locked. She'll have to come back when it's open and get that back. Christ, her grandmother gave her that cross on her deathbed!

Slightly miffed, April keeps walking. She passes the local bar and looks inside. An alcoholic is asleep on the counter. It's a rustic little tavern with a jukebox. She puts it on her list to visit later.

When she comes to the beach, she turns to the left and walks for a while picking up shells. She gets to the spit and crosses it. It's low tide. April walks out to the tip, feeling the sun on her face. It is strong and so is she. The winter is turning to spring. April spins.

And that's when she sees her boat, half a mile away, lying on its side. She is shocked. There's a gaping hole in it, and the sails are in shreds. Gulls and ravens are perched on what's left of the mast.

April starts making her way toward her yacht. She finds herself running and can feel her breasts brutally bouncing. It hurts when she runs, so she slows it down. Damn implants!

She reaches the wreck, and the birds take off, squawking at her. She looks into the hole and sees small crabs scuttling all over, then climbs inside and looks around. Eventually, her eyes adjust to the light. The boat is empty. No furniture, nothing. Even the lightbulbs have been unscrewed.

Could the sea have done this? No way. There are human scuff marks in the sand, and cig butts in the windowsills.

"C'est la vie," April tells her yacht, climbing out of it. She looks at the tide coming in, turns around, and looks toward the line where the wet sand meets the dry sand, up by the kelp buzzing with flies. No doubt the tide will take her ravaged craft away.

Oh well, she figures, she'll just have to get another one. April shrugs and heads to the market to buy some flowers for her yard.

10

Y ANN IS OFF AT SEA, sitting on the aft deck, playing his accordion. The other fishermen are in the
cabin cutting up lines of crank. They are heading
out for shark, which will be skinned and cleaned, ground
up into Puppy Chow, and listed as "cod" on the label.

Yann watches the island becoming smaller. Somewhere
on those shores, she is walking around with those lips —
those lips he cannot get out of his mind — unlike Nadine
and her big black bush, which doesn't tempt him anymore.
He's been there, and it was a nightmare.

April, however, is a woman! A beautiful woman, an incredible woman, a woman he could never think of doing
like he did Nadine. April is not that kind of person — she is
too good for such filth. Yann could see it in her eyes, the
way they shined when she smiled at him coming down the
hill that morning. Like an angel.

The island gets smaller and the lips get bigger. Those
luscious, perfect lips, floating on the horizon before him!
What he would give to kiss those lips! Maybe he'd even
give his life for a kiss. Just a kiss, to be graced by a kiss.

But this, of course, is what all the men want. Yann knows his visions are nothing special. They are all in love with April — she is the siren of the island. The fishermen have become respectful. They'd make comments about porking the Virgin from behind, but no such words are ever uttered of April, worshiped by all men.

What a gorgeous day, Yann thinks. It's the first warm day this spring. He takes off his shirt and lets the sun begin to burn his skin as he drifts with his music. Bubba used to call him a fag for playing the accordion, but nobody else ever complained. Radio reception isn't very good on the ocean, except for a couple of classic rock stations, which come in fuzzy, so the sailors always welcome the sound. Yann plays on.

Every song Yann plays is for April. He imagines himself serenading her. He imagines himself doing chores for her. He imagines himself at her feet. He wants to be her dog.

But then he begins to think again about Nadine. That was a complete mistake! He should never have gone to dinner at her place. Just thinking of that animal act makes the gall rise in his throat. Never again, he thinks. But still, it was good to get his rocks off . . .

At that very moment, Nadine is in the market picking through a pile of melons some ship from the South dumped on the island. She chooses one.

"Too ripe!" a crotchety voice tells her.

Nadine looks up. It's Mother Kralik, still pissed off about the cave. Nadine can tell from the tone of her voice. She ignores the old bag and puts the melon down. She picks up another one.

"Too young!" Mother Kralik snaps.

Nadine puts it down and goes for another.

"Too round!" Mother Kralik says with increasing disgust.

Defiantly, Nadine grabs a random melon. The moment she touches it, Mother Kralik's bony hand grabs the melon away from her. Nadine spins to face her.

Mother Kralik, however, doesn't say anything. She just holds the melon in front of her face and burns a scowl across its rind. She is breathing hard to control her rage, and her sinuses are whistling. Then she turns the melon over, revealing a dark, rotten bruise.

"Too bruised," Mother Kralik says, her nasty yellow tooth appearing for a second.

Nadine grabs for the melon, but Mother Kralik pulls it away. They stare each other down, their eyes burning with hatred. Mother Kralik smiles, but Nadine keeps her face emotionless. It's obvious who is playing with whom. Mother Kralik grunts, puts the melon back, and walks away.

Exhaling annoyance, Nadine goes back to picking through the pile. She picks a melon up and inspects it for faults. It passes the inspection. She places it in her basket and looks at the form pulling up alongside her. It's that rich bitch April, smiling at her.

Nadine is the youngest female April's met on the island so far, and intriguing for this reason. April also notes that Nadine's dress is green, whereas the surly old women smoking cigs across the pile are dressed in depressing brown and black.

Nadine smiles back, just to be polite. Why shouldn't she be polite? Especially since Mother Kralik, Widow O'Reilly,

Widow Flanahan, and her mother are watching? So she even embellishes it a bit, just to piss them off — to see her being friendly with the rich bitch.

To April, though, the smile is sincere, and there's something about all those teeth. April doesn't know it, but the reason many of the old people have lost their teeth and many of the younger ones have most of their teeth is toothpaste, which made its debut on the island in the sixties.

To Nadine, April's smile is insincere. To Nadine, April's smile is saying, "Hello, you simple little thing, with your simple little dress and your simple little tits, looking for some simple food to make a simple supper." Still, Nadine also recognizes something in April that is reaching out to communicate with her—probably because they're not so far apart in age.

April settles on a melon. But before she can pick it up, Nadine's hand gently lands on top of hers. They are both immediately conscious of this action, the heat of each other's flesh, and the fact that they are touching. Neither moves her hand.

Slowly, seductively, April raises her eyes from the melon and locks them questioningly on Nadine, who has a peculiar grin on her face. Nadine nods at the melon.

Spooning April's hand in hers, Nadine rotates the melon. A big, rotten bruise is revealed. It's the melon she and Mother Kralik had been squabbling over.

April sees the bruise and is appreciative. She flutters her eyelids a bit and nods thankfully, pursing her lips. Nadine's eyes respond to this, shining brightly back. She takes her hand off April's and reaches into her basket.

Without a word, Nadine take her own flawless melon out

and hands it to April, who accepts. They regard each other for an unusual amount of time, both of them grinning. And then, simultaneously, both of them burst out laughing, as if sharing a secret joke.

They laugh and laugh and laugh. They laugh up a storm, and every time they try to stop, they burst out guffawing again. They laugh until they cry, both of them holding their sides. April, however, has to reposition her hands to hold her crotch to keep herself from peeing. This makes them both laugh harder. They call attention to themselves.

"Great," Mother Kralik whispers to Widow Murphy. "Just great. Slut meets slut! Sluts laugh their asses off! Sluts become friends! Just perfect!"

Nadine's mother stares straight ahead. The other hags cackle with agreement.

"I'll tell you what," Mother Kralik continues, "that slut daughter of yours thinks she's really happy now. Oh yes, she's really really happy. She thinks she's found a friend. She might even have a bit of an eye for that hussy too. But I'll tell you what . . . that little slut of yours, she's only happy cuz she *thinks* she's equal with that rich bitch, but that's where she's wrong! Dead wrong!"

Widow Murphy starts to drool as Mother Kralik hawks up some phlegm, then spits it at her feet.

"I'll guarantee you this," Mother Kralik tells the hags, shaking her cig in Nadine's direction. "That rich bitch with the fat tits'll have that little slut washing her ass before too long! Yep, she'll be licking her ass, you just watch! I guarantee it—that's what always happens when slut meets slut! Mark my words. You'll see!"

Nadine and April begin to recover from their bout of laughter. They shake their heads and look at each other, too exhausted to start up again. If someone were to fart, they would both lose it completely — which is the look they are warning each other with: *Don't say anything funny!*

April leans forward and places a hand on Nadine's shoulder, and Nadine smiles back. It seems as if they're instant friends, because suddenly they hug—laughing about their laughter, but this time with a different laughter, more controlled, subdued.

"Gimme a fucking break," Mother Kralik says, flicking her butt onto the pavement.She turns and waddles away, and the other hags follow. Widow Murphy is left alone, a strand of saliva hanging from her chin.

II

A COUPLE OF AFTERNOONS LATER, Yann's boat comes back. They'd filled their boat with an unorthodox meat, in a not-too-orthodox way. After finding a spot with a lot of deep down activity on their fish radar, they dropped in a bunch of putrid cod carcasses weighted down by cinder blocks, and let it all sink to the bottom. Then they dropped in their blood bombs: fifty-five-gallon drums full of chum, sealed shut, then shot full of holes. The barrels sank, releasing bright clouds of fetid fluids, exciting the sharks into a frenzy. After enough were attracted, the fishermen dropped the depth charges in. When they hit the bottom and went off, hundreds of mud sharks, dogfish, manta rays, and skates floated toward the surface. The men up top shot all the injured fish and gathered the bodies blasted by the shock. Such fishing methods, of course, are illegal in international waters, but there is no authority in the vicinity to enforce anything — and, besides, who cares what dogs eat in Russia and Japan?

Hefting his duffel bag over one shoulder, his accor-

dion hanging on the other, Yann walks off the dock and
starts up the hill. There is one thought on his mind: April
Berger.

Then he sees Nadine coming straight for him with a
mop slung over her shoulder. He considers slipping behind
a Dumpster, but she has already spotted him. She is
marching furiously, with a pack of old women at her heels,
still dressed in their cannery smocks.

"Hey!" Mother Kralik calls out, twisting her wrists.
"Where you going, little miss scrub-bitch?! That sure is a
nice mop you've got there. Do you use that to douche the
rich bitch with?!"

"Yeah!" Widow O'Reilly puts in. "You better hurry up,
chop chop! Wouldn't want to upset the boss!"

"Hurry up, hurry up!" Widow Flanahan adds. "A ser-
vant's work is never done!"

Even Nadine's mother is there, following the women.
She isn't saying anything, but it's clear whose side she's on.

"Fuck all y'all!" Nadine screams, turning to face them.
She is only twenty steps from Yann. Then she throws her
mop at them, spins, runs to Yann, grabs his arm, and leads
him away. And he goes with her, so as not to further em-
barrass her.

"What was that all about?" Yann asks, as they round the
corner.

"They're just giving me shit because I gotta better job
than them," Nadine says, fuming.

"Doing what?"

"Working for April. She's living here on the island now,
you know. We hit it off the other day. Now we're tight."

Yann seems impressed, which, of course, is what Nadine was hoping for.

"So you, ummm . . . mop?" he asks.

"I do whatever she says to do," Nadine tells him. This isn't the direction she wanted their conversation to go. They stop in front of the post office. "She wants me to pick up her mail. C'mon."

Nadine leads Yann into the office. "I'm s'posed to pick up some packages for April Berger," Nadine tells the clerk.

"Ahh," he says, "the new girl. She's quite a popular gal. I've got some letters here for her too."

The clerk hands her a gargantuan bundle of envelopes bound by the largest rubber band Yann has seen in his life. He sets down his load as Nadine starts going through the letters, all of them with yellow forwarding stickers indicating a change of address. Nadine peels one back and sees an L.A. address. She starts reading the return addresses off: "New York, Minnesota, Colorado, Manitoba . . . London, Arizona, Toronto, Rhode Island . . . what's the deal with her?"

"Maybe she's gotta lotta pen pals," Yann suggests.

"Maybe the whole world knows who she is . . . and maybe we don't know shit!"

"I thought you guys were buddies."

Nadine doesn't comment. She continues to look through the pile as Yann shifts his weight from side to side, wondering what he's doing with this loon . . . who really doesn't have such a badly shaped ass . . .

The clerk comes back with four big boxes piled on a dolly. "Well," he says, "here's her mail. If you want to leave a couple and come back later —"

"No," Nadine says, placing the letters on the top box and hefting it off the pile, "we'll take them all now. Come on, Yann."

Nadine starts walking toward the door. For a second, Yann hesitates. He looks at the three big boxes, wondering if he can balance them all, then he looks at his stuff.

"Don't worry about your gear," the clerk tells him. "You can leave it here. I'll be open for another hour."

Yann nods and picks up the boxes. They wobble precariously, but he manages to follow Nadine out the door.

In the street Nadine picks up the pace, walking briskly up the hill. Yann struggles behind her, hardly able to see around his load. The wind is blowing hard, which doesn't make it any easier. They eventually make it to April's house.

April is out front kneeling by some tulips, a garden shovel in her hand. Next to her is a wheelbarrow full of flowers for planting. The ones that have already been planted are bending severely in the wind.

When April sees Nadine and Yann, she jumps up and brushes off her hands. "Oh goodie, goodie, goodie!" she sings.

Nadine hands April her bundle of letters. April looks at them, then tosses them into the wheelbarrow. She grabs the top box from Yann. "Oh thank you so much, Yann," she coos, "you're such a dear."

Nadine mimics April behind her back, but nobody sees this. Where April learned Yann's name, neither Nadine nor Yann knows. She must've asked around.

Meanwhile, April has already started tearing into the box. Yann sets the other two down.

"Oh look!" April gasps, producing a stuffed elephant. "It's Elphy! Oh, Elphy, I've missed you so!"

April starts dancing around the yard with Elphy. She sings to it. "Hi, Elphy, hi, Elphy, hi, Elphy . . . Oh, Elphy, Elphy, Elphy . . ."

Yann and Nadine turn toward each other and share a look of wary uncertainty. April goes back to the box and starts digging through it. She pulls out newspaper wads put in for packing, which are blown away by the wind when she drops them on the lawn.

"And look!" she cries, pulling out a stuffed rabbit. "Bun-bun's here too. Hi, Bun-bun!"

April makes Bun-bun do a little dance. Then she puts it in Yann's face and repeats the dance. Yann laughs, and she hands it off to Nadine, without even looking at her, and goes back to the box.

"And Brown Bear's here, and Pookie! My friends! My friends have come! It's been such a long time since I've seen them — well, that's not true. I did see them last Christmas, but that was . . . Oh, where's Bun-bun?"

April looks around for Bun-bun, then sees it in Nadine's hands.

"Oh, you're hurting Bun-bun!" she cries.

Everyone looks at Bun-bun. Nadine is wringing its neck.

"Oh, sorry," Nadine says, and hands it back to April, who dismisses this and repeats the Bun-bun dance.

"Hi, Bun-bun, how are you?" April asks it, then turns to Yann, who is showing some interest. "Bun-bun's the oldest of them all. When I was a little girl, Bun-bun used to have beads for eyes, but I think I accidentally swallowed one, so Mommy had these google-eyes sewn on. Not that I wouldn't've swallowed google-eyes, but I guess they didn't attract me as much. I mean, kids don't want to eat google-eyes, they want to eat candy!"

Yann is watching April's lips. They are opening and closing, opening and closing . . .

"And everyone knows that beads look more like candy than google-eyes do," April rambles on. "Don't you think so, Yann? Well, I can't really say for sure. Maybe candy these days looks more like google-eyes than beads do. I mean, candy can be gross these days. I remember this kind of candy that used to come in a little plastic trash can. Do you remember that stuff, it was called . . ."

Yann is staring hard at April, nodding at everything she says. Nadine wishes she had that stupid rabbit in her hands again.

"Garbage!" April says, "I think, or something like that. Maybe it was called Trash. I can't remember, it had like little sugar beer cans in it, and bad cabbage and stuff. But that's beside the point! The point being, I am so glad to have my *aminals* here! Didn't you used to have any *aminals* when you were a little boy, Yann? My big brother used to have a stuffed bat, if you can imagine that. I was the baby of the family if you haven't guessed already. It was actually a pretty cute bat, though . . . for a bat. My brother used to take that bat everywhere. That bat's name was Herman. Oh, you should meet my kitty, Poo-poo. Yoo-hoo, Poo-poo, where are you? I guess she's not around right now.

But back to Herman: Herman! Isn't that a wacky name for a bat?"

"Yeah," Yann agrees, totally involved in April's little-girl world. "Herman's a weird name . . . for a bat."

"No it ain't," Nadine breaks in. April and Yann turn toward her. By the startled expressions on their faces, it's as if they'd forgotten she was there.

"It's not a weird name," Nadine says, trying to control her rage. "It's a good name for a bat. All bats are named Herman."

Yann and April give each other a confused look. Then Yann sees something, and his eyebrows rise. He instantly becomes excited and starts to run in one direction but comically turns in the other. It's a Jerry Lewis move, but real. April laughs.

Yann runs over to the rock pile in the corner of the yard and gathers up an armful of rubble. He comes back, drops to his knees, and immediately starts constructing a windbreak around a flower that is being battered by the wind.

"Oh, Yanny!" April immediately shouts with glee. "How thoughtful of you!"

Nadine snarls and turns away. Nobody notices. She goes stomping out the gate and turns around. Still, they haven't noticed she's leaving. Yann is building another windbreak, and April is clasping her hands endearingly.

"You fucking rich bitch," Nadine sneers beneath her breath. "I'll . . . I'll . . . I'll . . ." But she can't think of what she'll do. And besides, she wouldn't have the courage to tell them anyway. So she clicks the gate shut and stomps off down the hill.

12

IN THE MORNING, having lain there half the night
staring at the ceiling, she knows she has to take action.
Nadine gets out of bed and affectionately addresses the
fetus she envisions inside her. "Don't worry, you little shit,
we'll get him yet."

Nadine wakes her mother up by kicking at her door, then
puts some water on to boil. She looks around at the
kitchen: it's a mess. Now that her mother is a virtual veg-
etable, nothing ever gets done around the house.

Her mother comes out, and they stare at each other.
"What the fuck are you looking at?" Nadine greets her and
makes the coffee. They sit down and glare across the table
at each other.

Later, as she's leading her mother to work (the factory having declared that any moron can sit on an assembly line),
her plan begins to form. By the time she drops her mother
off with Mother Kralik and the other widows, she knows
what she will say.

Determined, Nadine marches straight over to Yann's trailer and bangs on the door. Nobody answers. She shoves the door open. The place is dark and empty. It's seven in the morning; why wouldn't he be here? She's checked his schedule, and he isn't going out to sea for two more days.

"He's with that rich bitch," she tells her imaginary child and looks around for something to smash. She particularly wants to smash his accordion, but it isn't there. Nor is his bag.

"That fucking slut!" Nadine screams and goes for his toaster but stops herself. What's she going to do, toss it through the window? That might not look too good. Trembling, she turns and leaves.

Nadine sets a collision course with April's house but pauses when she gets to the post office. She looks through the window and sees Yann's duffel bag and accordion still there, where he left them the afternoon before.

"Rrrrr!" Nadine growls. She starts to wonder if she would really kill that rich bitch — because that's what she's seeing in her head: bursting through April's front door, charging up the stairs, she finds them together in bed, then goes to town with a machete! But first she has to get a machete.

Nadine decides to play it by ear. Maybe what she's thinking is not the way it is — which has happened before. She can feel the blood pulsing in her head as she nears April's fence.

And there he is, the big lout! On his hands and knees, patting the earth around a flower. April's yard is covered with flowers, hundreds of them: tulips, roses, lilies, blossoms of all sorts. And all of them protected by windbreaks made from rock.

Yann stands up and brushes the dirt off his hands. He's wearing a jacket, so he probably went home at some point. Plus, it looks like he went down to the market and picked up a couple more loads of flowers. He looks around, admiring his work.

"Hey," Nadine says, her voice cracking.

Yann is startled. He didn't know she was watching him.

"Well, how does it look?" he asks, gesturing around him.

"Why the hell did you do this?" Nadine demands.

"For the flowers," Yann cheerfully answers.

"The flowers?"

"Yeah, the flowers."

Nadine hesitates, then lets it out: "What are you?! Some sort of shithead?! You got shit for brains or something?! Where's your brain at?!"

Yann hears Bubba in Nadine and lowers his head. "I did it for the flowers," he guiltily replies.

"Cuz I'll be damned if I marry a goddamned shitfer-brains!" Nadine tells him.

"Marry?"

"Yeah! Marry! I mean, that's why we're together, ain't it? Don't go telling me you ain't fixing on marrying me! You fucked me, Yann. You fucked me good! Are you telling me that you fucked me and you never even wanted to marry me?! Is that what you're trying to tell me?!"

Yann raises his eyes. She's standing there with her hands on her hips, glaring bullets at him. Man, he never should have gone there.

"No," he says.

"Are you trying to tell me that all I am to you is some sleazy fish-town whore?! Is that what you're trying to tell me?!"

"No . . . I never said that . . ."

Then she drops the bomb. "Yann," she tells him, "you knocked me up!"

His jaw drops, his eyes go wide. "You? . . . how?"

"Cuz, Shitferbrains, you didn't fuck me in the fucking asshole like you should've! And you didn't wear no rubber! You fucked me in my fucking cunt, with fucking cum all over your rapist dick!"

Luckily for Yann, nobody is up or out on the streets to hear this. Especially April.

"But that was just a few days ago . . ."

"Are you calling me a liar? Don't you think a woman knows her own body better than some man?! Are you saying you know my body better than me?! Haw! How dare you stick your slimy dick in me and cream and get me preggy, then go and call me a liar?!"

"I'm not saying that . . ."

"Come here!"

Yann obeys and walks up to the fence.

"From now on we're engaged! Got it?"

"Engaged?"

"Yes! Now get down on your knees and do it proper!"

Yann figures he can do it, or not do it. If he does it, maybe she'll shut up and he can think about this, and figure something out. But if he doesn't do it, then she's gonna fly off the handle and wake April up. But he'd rather have her just calm down, because it means more for him to please

April than it does for him to please Nadine — who is obviously delusional anyway.

Knowing he's fucking up, Yann gets down on his knees.

"That's right," Nadine says, "on your knees, scumdog! Now do it! Fucking propose to me!"

Yann crosses his fingers behind his back. Nobody would ever believe her anyway. Besides, if it came to that, he'd lie. He has no intention of marrying her — which is the truth he will swear by.

"Ummm . . . since you're gonna be a mom, and cuz I'm gonna be a dad . . . I guess —"

"Just fucking say it!"

Yann is glad she's on the other side of the fence, because if anybody saw this it would look like he was working on the flowers.

"Ummm . . . will you like . . . like marry me, Nadine?"

"Yes! Now stop gruvling around and get up, and give me a proper engagement-type kiss, Godfuckingdammit!"

Yann stands up and hesitates. He waits a few seconds, wondering if he should. Nadine's eyes get angrier and angrier. Then they both hear April behind them.

"Yoo-hoo," she calls, "good morning!"

They turn and see her in her doorway, holding her kitten. She's in her bathrobe and not too awake yet. She steps out on the porch and looks around.

"Oh my God, Yanny!" she says. "What did you do? Oh, Poo-poo, look what he did! The yard looks gorgeous! Oh, Yanny! You sweet, sweet man! I had no idea you were out here all night! Oh, it looks fantastic, I'm so touched! What a sweet, sweet gesture!"

Nadine looks to Yann. He's wearing a very dumb-looking grin, staring dreamily at April. Nadine starts to fume so hard she surprises herself by not exploding.

"Oh," April says, "and there you are too, Nadine, just in time. I was thinking you could do the windows today. There's a bucket in the bathroom upstairs and some Windex too. I've got some rags under the sink. After that, I'll find some other chores for you. Don't you think the yard looks great?"

"Yeah," Nadine says, swinging open the gate. She goes up to April, walks past her and into the house. She finds herself heading upstairs to start work but goes to the window to spy before she begins.

Down below April is jabbering away at a hundred miles an hour, and Yann is staring at her. He's focused on her lips, but Nadine thinks it's her tits. She sees April put down the cat, run into the house, then run back with her purse. She pulls out some bills.

"Come on, Yann," she says, holding the money toward him, "take the money. Take it for the work you've done. You've been so good, take the money. Come on, take it! It's nothing to me, I'm sure you could use it more than me."

Yann shakes his head, refusing. He looks at his shoes and doesn't say anything, while Nadine restrains herself from opening the window and yelling down at him, "Take the money, you idiot! We're gonna need diapers!"

Then she sees April put her hands on her hips and playfully admonish Yann. He still won't accept the money — and Nadine hopes this is because he's so absorbed in his engagement that he can't think straight. But then April saunters toward him like the whore she is and suddenly throws her arms around him. "You're a wonderful, wonderful man, Yann," she tells him and kisses him on the cheek. Nadine sees her slide the money into his back pocket and slap him on the ass.

At this point, Nadine sees red. She's heard the expression before, but now she's finding out what it means. Everything goes bright, dark red — and she feels a twitching in her neck. A twitching that could take her over if she let it.

"Rrrrrr!" Nadine growls. If she doesn't smash something soon, who knows what she'll do?

April's kitten trots into the room and rubs up against her. Purring, it looks up at Nadine, so trusting and small and fragile. She bends down and picks it up.

"Hi, kitty," Nadine says.

13

NADINE IS BEHIND THE HOUSE cleaning windows again. She speaks to herself as she sprays and wipes, with jerky, erratic motions, mocking her employer. "Oh, and after you do the laundry, Nadine, then you can scrub the bathroom, Nadine . . . and oh, after you do the laundry, Nadine, then you can polish the floor, Nadine . . . and oh, after you polish the floor, Nadine, you can wash the windows again, Nadine, they just need a little touching up, you missed some spots the other day. You *are* happy with your job, aren't you? I *am* paying you enough, aren't I?"

She feels a spasm in her neck. Lately, this has been an increasing occurrence—something she is getting used to. Like taking her mother to Mother Kralik every morning, and picking her up every evening, and those glares they give each other across the table, neither of them saying anything to the other, just eating and seething.

And Yann! Where the hell is he? He's off at sea playing around, probably fucking some whore! Or planning his escape. He never comes by to see her. He doesn't give a fucking shit!

Nadine squeezes the spray bottle like she's choking a chicken, over and over again. She doesn't even know it, but she just sprayed half the Windex on the window. She looks at it and lets it drip. About the only thing that gives her pleasure these days is the fact that April is still upset about her missing kitten.

In the window Nadine can see her reflection grinning back like a sicko, distorted by the ripples running down the glass. And she likes the way she looks.

Nadine wipes the Windex off and hooks the bottle under the sash of her dress, tucking a rag in also. She starts to climb. The trellis takes her to the second story. This is how she got to the upstairs window a few days before.

Nadine gets to the bedroom window and looks in. She's surprised to see April there, thinking that she'd gone to the market. But nope, she's there, with her big stick-out tits, sitting on the bed, opening the package she just picked up at the post office.

From where Nadine is kneeling, she knows that April can't see her, so she decides to take a break. She wants to see what's in the box that's making April smile so hard. Then she sees why. The package is on the floor, and April is holding a big knobby dildo in her hand.

"Holy fuck," Nadine whispers. She knows what it is from looking in her father's nudie magazines — which she sold to some pervert sailor for ten bucks. The whole collection.

April wastes no time in seducing the thing. She places it

on the bed, then starts strutting around in front of it, glancing at it now and then with a coy, sassy look. Then, when April begins unbuttoning her blouse, Nadine pulls back a few more inches just to make sure she won't be seen. She knows she is in for a show.

Button by button, April's blouse comes undone. And then it's off, and she's standing there, posing for the dildo with a lacy white bra on, restraining those big honking hooters.

Nadine bites her lower lip. April is indeed a foxy lady.

Then April steps out of her skirt. She's wearing some panties that are equally sexy. They're the kind that go right up the crack of her ass — so there's a lot of long, lean flank in the air. And whatta bumper!

Nadine is surprised to feel her nipples tingle. What is she, some sort of lesbo? Hell no! She knows she's not that — otherwise she would've kept them pornos. She is hot for Yann's cock, goddammit!

But so is April, which is why she's strutting around in front of the dildo, showing it her ass and shaking her tits in its face. This lasts another couple minutes. Then, *snap,* she unclasps her bra, and her boobs pop out. Nadine can't believe it. Now they're even bigger than before. How the fuck does she carry those around?

April grasps a breast in each hand and starts squeezing, trying to entice the dildo. She hoists a breast up to her lips and starts to lick the nipple. Nadine watches as it becomes erect.

Then April lies down on her back, on the bed, next to the dildo. She peels off her panties, her feet toward Nadine. Slowly they begin to part. A few seconds later Nadine is staring into a wide-open beaver, surrounded by a nicely groomed, petite yellow bush — which isn't all big and overgrown like her trashy black gash — as her father used to call it.

Nadine watches as April licks a finger and gently begins to frig herself. Running her fingertip up and down her labial lips, she occasionally moans, then settles on the clitoris tip, at the top of her glistening slit. And right beneath that: her asshole.

Then Nadine hears vibrations. It isn't just a dildo, it's a vibrator, and April knows how to use it. She is rubbing it and rubbing it and rubbing it against her, and tossing her head from side to side, sometimes lifting her ass off the bed.

Nadine can't help it. Since she discovers that she's diddling herself, and since she knows she's wet, she inserts her thumb into her cunt and begins to press on the place she believes is her G-spot.

Now April's motions are getting faster. Not only can Nadine see April's hot twat getting jerked off but her asshole is opening and closing beneath it — and this, for some reason, makes Nadine hot.

Fucking A, Nadine thinks, that rich bitch sure looks like a million bucks . . .

Not only is April's pussy dripping wet and ready for fucking but her tits are in the air and her nipples are as hard as rocks. And so are Nadine's.

If I was in there, Nadine thinks, I'd be getting down between them legs. I'd be slurping her like a Popsicle.

But April refuses to plunge it in. She just holds it there on top of her clit and lets it hum away. It hums in time with her breathing, which Nadine can hear — and so she times her own exhalations to April's. Both of them are going for it, working something up: something hot and slippery, something deep and wet inside.

Nadine feels her fist pounding her pubic mound. Her thumb is squishing around. She has never been so turned on in her life, not even with Yann. Christ! Maybe she goes both ways.

But still, April won't fuck herself. Nadine has to keep from shouting out advice. April is being all delicate and shit. She holds the vibrator tip against her lips and tickles herself like a tease.

Nadine, however, wants it hard and fast. She starts thumping and thumping, banging and banging her fist against her cunt, her thumb going in and out of her slickened lips, a grimace affixed to her face.

Meanwhile, April, on the bed, is tossing her head back and forth, gaining momentum. And then she lifts the vibrator up and points it straight down, its tip poised on the apex of her sex. Nadine hopes she'll stuff that sucker in and get fucked, but again, she won't. She just holds it there as her asshole starts quirking like a little mouth whistling some tune. And then April comes, groaning softly.

Nadine, however, can't get off, even though she is pounding and pounding away at herself. "Come on," she whispers to her cunt, gritting her teeth. "Come on, you piece of shit!" But she can't. She has to have something in her ass.

"Goddamn you," she whispers to her anus, then takes her thumb out and grabs the squirt bottle and spits on the nozzle. She shoves it up her ass. It hurts, but not that bad. She crams it in as far as it will go but doesn't pull the trigger. If she did that, she'd shoot ammonia into her colon, and that probably wouldn't feel too good.

April is lying there breathing hard, her tits heaving up and down. Nadine is jamming and ramming herself. She feels a giant b.m. coming but keeps on going anyway. She can see her reflection in April's window. She's all clenched up and furious, and about to come. She is on the edge. Shit is gonna fly!

And that's when April sits up in bed, and Nadine thinks she might be seen. So she pulls back and pulls out. And since she knows she isn't going to come, she decides to fake it for herself, so lies back against the shingles and pretends to sigh, imitating the lift and swell of April's breasts — but quietly.

A few seconds later, Nadine can hear April rustling around, getting her clothes back on. Then she hears the door open and close, so she scrambles down the trellis and pretends to be hard at work.

April comes around the corner, a healthy, refreshed glow on her face. "Hey, Nadine," she says, with a strange, twisty curve in her voice. Nadine wonders if this is some sort of a hint that she knows she was watching.

"Hey, April." Nadine smiles back. "What's up?"

"Oh nothing," April says and stares back at Nadine, flashing her lashes, then looking around. "I just feel wonderful today. How do you feel?"

"I feel great," Nadine finds herself replying, as she regards her employer with a similar look. She wants to rip April's clothes off and bend her over from behind. She'll lick her rich bitch ass, then shove the Windex nozzle up it. Her cute little asshole! Her cunt!

"But," April says, with a sudden inflection of melancholy, "you haven't seen Poo-poo around, have you?"

"No," Nadine answers, affecting a sympathetic voice. She is imagining how she'll stuff April's face into the pillow and slap her ass from behind.

Each takes a step toward the other.

"I . . . I" — April is trying to say something — "I miss Poo-poo so much."

It's obvious: they're going to hug. Nadine grips the spray bottle tighter. But when they wrap their arms around each other, she drops it to the ground.

April presses her body against Nadine's; her breasts are practically in her face. Nadine places her hand on April's ass. They hold each other for a minute, then April pulls back.

"Poor little Poo-poo," April says, with a slight sniffle, "wandering the island all by herself, looking for her mommy."

"Don't worry," Nadine comforts her. "I'm sure you'll see her again one day."

"Well," April says, wiping a tear off her cheek, "I guess I'll go down to the market now. I'm gonna go try to find that Mother Kralik; she's got something in her store I want."

"She won't be there," Nadine finds herself telling April,

"because she's at work and her store won't open for a few more weeks. And then it's only open in the evenings."

"Well," April says, "then I guess I'll go for a walk."

"Okay," Nadine says and watches her start to walk off. But right when April is about to round the corner, she pauses and turns toward Nadine. "Hey, Nadine," she asks, "do you wanna have a drink later on? I could use the company."

"Sure," Nadine replies, feeling all fluttery inside. "What time?"

"Oh, how about happy hour? Do they have a happy hour down at that lounge?"

"No," Nadine says. "What's a happy hour?"

April laughs at that. "Oh, Nadine, you're just too much. Why don't we just meet there after you get off work . . . around six?"

"I'd love to," Nadine says, as if accepting a date.

April smiles, nods, and walks off as Nadine stoops over to pick up the Windex.

"She wants it," she tells the squirt bottle and gets back to work, wondering what she could possibly wear.

14

FTER A COUPLE of covert masturbations, Nadine finishes her work, then goes home and gets off again, this time with some help from the cork handle of a fishing pole. Every time she's about to come, a white-hot flash appears in her mind, and in that heat, visions of April and Yann intertwine. Either Yann is jerking off or April is frigging away. But they're never doing it together. It's either one image or the other.

Nadine has never been so horned up in all her life. She figures she better wear some panties for her big date, because she's been getting so wet. A spot on her dress would surely turn April off.

Nadine starts getting gussied up. She puts on mascara, lipstick, rouge, and covers up some zits. Then she puts on a bra and pads it with bum wad. After that, she picks out a dress that's way too tight but decides she can suck it in. She doesn't know the buttons are straining in back, and crescents of flesh can be seen running up her spine.

Then she goes into the kitchen. Her mother is sitting there smoking cigs with Mother Kralik, who immediately takes an interest in Nadine's appearance. "Oh," the old crone says, with less sarcasm than usual, "so you're all dolled up tonight, huh? Who's the lucky sailor?"

Nadine considers lying and telling them it's Yann, but she knows she might get busted.

"April," she says.

"Oh," Mother Kralik says, raising her eyebrows and turning toward Widow Murphy, sitting there like a mannequin. "It looks like your daughter has made a new friend . . . her employer."

Nadine's mother says nothing, but stares straight ahead. It's the same thing she does at work all day — just stares at a conveyor belt, watching for mislabeled cans, which constantly pass by. The factory, however, doesn't care. They are required to have inspectors on all outgoing products, no matter their competence level.

"We're gonna go get a drink," Nadine tells Mother Kralik, with no emotion whatsoever. It appears their anger at each other has abated.

"That's nice," Mother Kralik condescends, sneering only slightly. "She seems like a very nice girl . . . maybe I misjudged her."

Nadine doesn't say anything. She puts some white bread in the toaster and waits. She'll need to eat something before she goes out boozing.

The toast pops up, and Nadine places it on the counter, then sprays it with butter-flavored Pam. It's her favorite snack. She takes it and starts heading toward the door.

"Tell April hello," Mother Kralik says to Nadine as she opens the screen door.

"Yeah, right," Nadine mutters and steps out. She aims

herself toward the port and comes upon that smart-ass kid with the Clapton shirt. He's standing in the street poking at a dead rat with a stick.

"If you're looking for the rest of the clowns," he tells her, "the circus went the other way."

She gives him the finger and looks for something to hit him with. There's nothing but the stick he's holding, unless she wants to look like a stereotype and hit him with her purse. Nadine grabs for the stick, but the kid runs away. "Haw haw, clown-face, haw haw!"

Nadine feels a twitch in her neck but keeps on walking anyway. She makes it to the Dirty Dawgfish.

April, already, is seated inside. She's sitting at the bar with a couple of drinks in front of her. There's nobody else in the place except the bartender.

"Hi," Nadine says, grabbing a squat beside her.

"Nadine!" April gasps. "What happened to your face?"

"Whattya mean, what happened to my face?" she demands.

"Come with me," April says and grabs her hand. She leads Nadine to the ladies' room, where they shut the door behind them. It smells like piss in there.

"What am I going to do with you?" April asks and takes some toilet paper off the roll. "Your makeup is a mess. Here, hold still."

April comes at Nadine with the wad of t.p. and starts dabbing at her face.

"Fuck," Nadine whispers, shoulders sagging.

"Don't worry," April tells her, a bit unsteady on her feet, "I'm going to fix you up."

April wipes off virtually all the makeup Nadine applied, then takes out some of her own and starts putting it on her. For the second time in her life, Nadine sees red.

"Hmmm, I don't think you'll need any rouge," April says, "but maybe this eyeliner will help."

Then, after the makeup is reapplied, Nadine looks in the mirror. April has hardly done anything, and all her zits are visible now. Unlike April — who has perfect skin! Skin she'd like to —

"Oh my God," April tells her.

"Now what?" Nadine asks, not making any attempt to hide her irritation.

"Well," April says, "it's your dress. Don't you have a better one?"

"N-n-n-no!" Nadine stammers. "This is my best dress."

"Well it's all misbuttoned and stretched out in back," April tells her. "Here, I'll fix it."

April goes to work fixing the dress. Nadine has never been so humiliated in all her life.

"That's about as good as it'll get," April tells her, now paying attention to her own reflection. "I'll have to give you some of those dresses I threw under the sink. Look, the best thing for you to do is keep your back to the wall. It's no big deal, you'll be all right. Just stick with me, kid."

April laughs at her own joke and primps herself a bit. Nadine is silent and withdrawn. Now April will never let her fuck her. Maybe she'll have to take the bitch by force . . .

"Come on," April says, dancing out of the shitter, wiggling her ass, "we've got a buzz to catch. Yaaa-hooo!"

Nadine follows April to the bar and tries to turn her back to the wall. The bartender immediately brings April a fancy yellow drink with an umbrella in it.

"Oh, thank you, Hans," April tells him, and he bows flamboyantly.

"Whatta ya want?" Hans asks Nadine, not even looking at her.

"A Bud."

Hans disappears.

"Oh, I just love this place," April says, swiveling around on her stool. "The decor is so authentic, and the people are so nice and friendly. Hans has been giving me free drinks for the last half hour."

Hans comes back and places a beer in front of Nadine. "Two bucks," he says.

"Oh!" April suddenly exclaims. "The jukebox! I almost forgot!"

April jumps up and starts dancing across the room, even though there isn't any music. Hans watches her, nodding his head in approval while Nadine digs through her purse, producing two crumpled dollar bills. She places them on the counter.

"Thanks," Hans says, scooping them up. He goes to the cash register, and April comes back. She leans forward, close to Nadine, and whispers, nodding toward the bartender. "He's got a nice butt, don't you think?"

Nadine looks over her shoulder and checks out his ass. "It's okay," she tells April, "but there are better buns on the island."

"That's for sure," April agrees. "He's not really my type anyway."

"And what *is* your type?" Nadine asks, no humor in her voice.

At that moment the music starts up. It's Bad Company, singing about some kid named Johnny who bought himself a six-string and set out to become a rock-and-roll star.

"Yessss!" April shouts, shaking it. "Come on, Nadine, let's dance."

April pulls Nadine off her stool and out in front of the jukebox. Nadine tries to imitate what April is doing but doesn't do a very good job. April notices that Nadine can't dance worth shit so leads her back to the bar.

"I just love classic rock," April says and downs half her drink. "It's so . . . so . . . I don't know . . . Classic!"

Nadine chugs her beer and orders another. Hans brings it and waits for another two bucks. The song ends and another one starts up. Some Aerosmith hit. April can't help it, she starts shaking it again.

Hans is mesmerized. "Whatta woman," he says to Nadine.

"Yeah," Nadine agrees, not knowing whether she'd rather get between those tits or lop them off with a cleaver.

The door swings open, and a bunch of fishermen walk in. Grisly old One Eye is leading the pack, and all of them are wearing crisp new shirts.

"So you can carry 'em around like a six-pack!" he yucks, delivering the punch line to some joke. The men burst out laughing.

And that's when they see April getting down on the dance floor. They immediately hush up and concentrate on her, simultaneously heading for the bar. When they get there, One Eye isn't looking, and he bumps into Nadine.

"Sorry, pal," he tells her, not even looking, and keeps on moving. They all sit down on the other side of her.

April comes back with beads of sweat forming on her chest. She unbuttons a button and lets her cleavage breathe. "Wow," she tells Nadine, "it feels so excellent to dance. I really miss my CD's."

"CD's?" Nadine asks. She's clueless about the term.

"Yeah," April says, guzzling her drink. She finishes it, and sets it down just as another arrives, compliments of Hans. This drink is served in a fancy coconut-looking cup.

"Oh, Hans, what service!" April gleefully tells him and leans across the bar, planting a kiss on his cheek. "That's so sweet!"

Nadine rolls her eyeballs, then suddenly remembers about her dress. All six fishermen next to her can see her back. She immediately stands up and walks to the other side of April.

"Where are you going?" April asks in astonishment, swaying a bit because of the liquor. "You aren't leaving me here, are you?"

"Uh, no," Nadine says. "I thought maybe it would be better if we sat over there, at that table, you know, by the wall."

"Nonsense," April says and grabs her wrist. "You sit right back down. This is where the action is!"

The next thing Nadine knows, April is guiding her back to her stool and sitting her butt down. What is she supposed to do? Resist? Nadine settles shamefully back on the stool, hunkering over the bar. No doubt all the fishermen are laughing at her dress. She decides to lump it.

"So how do you like it here, miss?" One Eye asks across Nadine.

"I love it!" April cries and jumps up and throws her arms wide. "I love it, I love it, I love it!"

"We're glad you like it," another fisherman says. "We don't get many nice folks like you moving to the island."

"Oh come on!" April waves her hand, stumbling back a step. Immediately, all six fishermen leap to their feet—but Hans reaches her first. He places a hand on her arm to steady her.

"Oh thanks." April laughs, and continues to laugh. Then all the fishermen laugh with her, sitting back down on their stools.

"Have you visited the lovely beaches of our fair island yet?" One Eye asks, as Nadine turns to sneer at him. He, as well as the other fishermen, is putting on a show. They never speak like this, using words like *lovely* and *nice*. In fact, hardly a sentence escapes their filthy mouths without the word *fuck* in it.

One Eye, however, keeps on acting like he's wearing a halo, smiling graciously at April. "Well," he tells her, "if you'd ever like a personal tour, please do let me know. I'd be glad to show you all the coves, many of which are ideal for swimming in the unseasonably warm tides of the island."

"How cavalier of you." April nods, sits back down, and sips her drink.

"Name's Gaston," One Eye says, reaching a hand across Nadine. "Gaston Lawless. Barkeep, another drink for the lady, on me."

He ain't no Gaston, Nadine thinks, he's fucking One Eye the fucking loser.

"Pleased to meet you," April answers back. Handshakes and names are exchanged all around. Nadine, of course, is left out.

Yann would never treat me like this, she thinks — then remembers that Yann and "Gaston" are on the same boat. If these assholes just got in, that means Yann is back on the island.

"I'm leaving," Nadine whispers to April, but April doesn't hear her. She's too busy flirting with Hans, so Nadine waits to get a word in edgewise.

"Your yard looks divine," a fishermen breaks in. It's that asshole she sold her father's pornos to. "Did you have it professionally landscaped?"

"Oh, you flatterer, you," April says. "No. It was Yann. He stayed up all night long out of the goodness of his heart, and did it for me."

Nadine hates the tone of April's voice, as well as the fakey fishermen, who nod approvingly toward each other, cocking their heads and lifting their chins and making such polite conversation.

They talk for an hour about nothing — all of them except Nadine, sipping her Bud and watching them. April is really starting to piss her off, acting ditzier than usual. Nadine, however, decides to stick it out — because then maybe she can get in April's pants.

After her fifth or sixth drink, April leans forward and whispers to Nadine, "These locals are so adorable. . . . I'm so lucky to have ended up here! I guess it's another case of being in the right place at the right time."

"I wonder where Poo-poo is, though," Nadine whispers back, just to bring her down a notch.

"Yes, you're right," April says. "I suppose I ought to head back, in case she's waiting for me. She's probably at home right now, waiting for her mommy."

The women rise to leave, amidst the objections of the men. April, however, promises to grace them with her presence again. They walk out into the cooling, darkening dusk, April swaying drunkenly, Nadine sober, and sharp as a blade.

15

"I DON'T FEEL TOO GOOD," April tells Nadine, weaving up the street back to her place.

"I'll walk you home," Nadine says, even though it's obvious that this is what is happening. What she really wants to do is see if April will invite her in so she can get some. But still, there's something else she really wants: to lay down the law about Yann.

"Umm," Nadine says, and takes a deep breath, causing a button to pop on her dress. "What do you think of Yann?"

"Yann? I think he's a hunk."

"Yeah, me too," Nadine agrees. "I'm so glad he's mine."

"What?" April asks, steadying herself and staring at Nadine — who keeps separating into two Nadines, then merging back to one.

"Me and Yann," Nadine answers, "have been doing it for a while . . . so like, uhhh . . . he proposed to me and I said yes."

"You're kidding," April says, trying to bring Nadine into focus.

"No, it happened right on your lawn."

April wavers for a bit, squinting at Nadine. Her vision comes into focus. Nadine's neckline has shifted, and her bra is visible now. There's a piece of tissue peeking from it. April wonders if she should tell Nadine or not.

Nadine, for her part, can't understand why April's taking so long to respond. She figures that April's getting ready to tell her she isn't worthy of him. If she says it, Nadine thinks, I'll deck her right here in the street.

April, however, surprises Nadine by answering in a sincerely happy tone: "Oh, Nadine, you caught yourself one hell of a man. I'm so happy for you!"

"You are?"

"Yes," April responds, feeling something going on in her gut. "He's wonderful . . . you're so lucky, Nadine. I'll tell you what . . . if he wasn't taken, I'd be all over him, he's so . . . so . . . so . . . so totally awesome!"

"I'm gonna keep him forever," Nadine replies. "No one will ever come between me and him — he's my totally awesome hunk."

"Nadine," April says, starting to choke, "you gotta . . . gotta hang on to that man . . . you gotta hang on to him like he's your own child! You gotta keep him happy and do whatever he wants you to . . . I mean, you gotta do everything you gotta do to keep him, because if you don't . . . there's plenty of women who will —"

"He won't go with any other women," Nadine says. "He'll only be with me. He loves me, he'd kill for me. And I'd do the same for him."

April laughs, even though something is rising inside her. She covers her mouth, then removes her hand for a second.

"I think I'm gonna get sick," April tells Nadine, then

steps forward, drops to her knees, and pukes in the street. Nadine stands above her, proud of the effect of her news.

April pukes again, then a third time. After that she wipes her chin and sits there breathing heavily for a while.

"Are you okay?" Nadine asks.

"Huh?" April asks, shocked to find she's not alone. She doesn't know where she is, or who she's talking to. When she looks at the form hovering above her, all she sees is a blur. Gradually, though, it comes into focus. It's Nadine.

"Jesus," April says, "I must've blacked out or something."

"You barfed," Nadine tells her.

"I did?"

"Yes, don't you remember? It happened just a minute ago."

April looks down and sees the puddle of vomit, and it makes her want to upchuck again. She stands and starts to stumble up the hill. She doesn't remember puking, she doesn't remember anything. All she knows is her throat is burning.

"How much did I drink tonight?" April asks.

"Five or six," Nadine says.

"Five or six what?"

"I don't know . . . fancy drinks."

April starts digging through her purse. She gets a pack of Tic Tacs out and pops a bunch in her mouth.

"Mint?" April asks, offering the package to Nadine.

"Naw," Nadine says, with annoyance. "You do remember what we were talking about, don't you?"

April begins to swoon again. The blood is pulsing in her

head. She looks at Nadine, whose mouth is opening and closing like a carp sucking scum off the surface of a pond. April figures that Nadine is asking her if she needs any help getting home.

"Yes," April answers. She reaches out for Nadine, and Nadine is there, supporting her. April shuffles along, in and out of vertigo. Nadine helps her up the hill.

Nearing April's house, they begin to hear accordion music. Yann is sitting on April's front porch with a plain white T-shirt on. His biceps are pumping away as he squeezes on his squeeze-box.

"Yanny!" April sings, suddenly breaking from Nadine. She lurches toward her fence and goes running into her yard, wiggling her ass like she did down in the bar — overcome by a burst of drunken energy.

"Wooo-hooo!" she cries. "Play it, Yanny!"

Nadine follows April into the yard but stops in the shadows. She looks at Yann's shirt and knows it's new. The fucker! What's come over all these men?

Yann has started on an old sailor's song of the island called "Shandy." April squeals with delight and starts twirling like a drunken high school girl.

Yann sings:

> Oh Shandy, she came one day
> to a lonely port in a lonely bay
> where the old salts fish
> and their women slave
> to make it through the day.
> Aye, to make it through the day . . .

"Rock on, Yann!" April cries, stumbling over one of the windbreaks Yann constructed in the yard. She keeps on dancing, throwing her arms into the air and prancing around like a prima donna.

Yann sings on:

> Oh Shandy was a bawdy lass
> with a curvy stern
> and a healthy yearn
> for sailors such as Bart.
> Aye, for sailors such as Bart.

April's balance begins to get better as her dance becomes increasingly erotic. She struts around like a bitch in heat.

> Now Bart was built
> like a sturdy scow
> with a prominent prow,
> which made the ladies swoon.
> Aye, it made the ladies swoon.

"Yo ho ho!" April breaks in with the chorus, swinging her hips like a fag in drag while Yann grins away like an idiot.

Nadine feels her neck start to twitch. Shit, it's happening again! She fucking hates that bitch!

Yann picks up the tempo:

> So when Shandy did see
> young Bart back from sea
> and the bulge in his bilge
> she released a gasp
> with both hands clasped
> and a burning in her breast.
> Aye, a burning in her breast.

Nadine's neck starts spazzing out. She puts a hand up to conceal her throat, but it doesn't matter. All eyes are on April, now doing a pole dance with one of the columns on her porch, as Yann keeps going:

> "Now Shandy lass," this lad did say,
> "you're quite a fine sight today.
> May I take you for a sail?
> Aye, may I take you for a sail?"

Nadine's neck is freaking her out. It hurts. What the hell is wrong with her?! Why won't the fucker stop?!

"Yo ho ho," April sings, really getting into it. "Ho ho ho!" Yann steps it up even more:

> So off they went in a summer squall
> which mattered none at all
> for the swell of the sea
> was something to see
> as she lay there in the hold.
> Aye, she lay there in the hold.

"Yo ho ho!" April puts in, then sways up to Yann and shakes her tailfeathers in his face. Yann laughs and grins a great big shit-eater toward Nadine, even though he doesn't know she's there. He can't see anything in the shadows.

> "Oh Shandy girl, the wind's picking up,"
> the hardy seaman told his maid
> as he dropped his jib
> and she lowered her sails.
> Aye, she lowered her lovely sails.

Nadine, meanwhile, is positive that Yann is smiling at her, making fun of her struggle with her neck. He's laughing at her — and she can't do a thing to stop it! Her muscles are jerking away on their own. Tears stream down her face. She's in its power! It's got her! She's toast!

Nadine can't take it anymore. She has to get the fuck out! She turns and bolts, leaving them together — Yann still singing gleefully:

> So they tossed and they turned
> as the ocean churned
> splashing the lovers
> from ankle to neck
> as the rollers rolled over the deck.
> Aye, the rollers rolled over the deck.

"The rollers rolled over the deck," April repeats, singing along, her ass eclipsing his face.

> "Bart my love, we're going down,"
> the saucy lass cried through the storm,
> and "Aye my love, I know," he replied
> for down he had already gone
> till up he came
> and slipped in his mast
> making it fast
> while waves washed over the hull.
> Aye, the waves washed over the hull.

April dances around Yann and comes up behind him. She presses down on his shoulders, and his muscles turn her on. She caresses the back of his neck.

"Yo ho ho," she sings, *"Ho ho ho!"*

> And they might've prayed
> and they might've swum
> but the tide was rising in Shandy

as their vessel went down
and down and down
for both were feeling randy.
Aye, both were feeling randy!

April comes around in front of Yann and pretends to fall into his lap. He stops playing, and both of them laugh. Yann puts his accordion away, and then it's silent.

For a few seconds they stare at each other. Yann is transfixed by her lips — those lips he's seen at sea consuming the horizon — those lips that have become his only goal in life — to press to his . . .

April is breathing hard from dancing. Her chest is heaving. Her eyes are shut, and her arms are reaching up. They find his head and start to pull it down. Her lips — those lips — they part. Yann can see the tip of her tongue. Her mouth opens like a flower. It is her entire person. He lowers his lips toward hers.

"Hic!" April hiccups and instantly passes out.

Yann stares at the woman on his lap, and those lips he must kiss or go nuts. Easily, he could sneak a kiss. Easily, he could wake her up, and she would not object. Either that or he could do the gentlemanly thing.

Which he does. He carries her up to her bed, takes off her shoes, and tucks her in. And he doesn't even kiss her good night.

16

HALF-STOMPING, HALF-RUNNING, Nadine and her neck storm through the night. She goes down to the beach, grabbing at her tendons, trying to stop them. Falling to the sand, she grapples with her throat as if it's something separate from her — as if she could strangle it into submission. Eventually, though, the twitching subsides.

Nadine sits up, covered with sand and bits of ground shell. She stares out at the half-moon rising above the horizon. There's enough moonlight for her to see the beach. There's a stick next to her. She grabs it like a dagger and drops her eyes toward the sand.

"Sand," she says, "such nice . . . nice sand . . . such perfect, smooth . . . sand."

She jabs the sand, then does it again. She slits it from its anus to its thorax, then tears its belly open, gouging at its innards. She disembowels the sand, leaves it gutted like a slime-line cod, then stands up and spits on it.

Nadine screams at the sea, a bloody murderous incensed

scream. She screams so hard it feels like flesh is ripping in her throat. And the more it hurts, the more sense it makes to keep on screaming. Maybe the pain will rip her gorge wide open, and then her demons will escape.

"Shut the fuck up!" some voice cries out from the silhouette of a trailer parked on the beach. It's a woman's duty to submit. Her mom always told her to keep her mouth shut when getting raped and pretend she was somewhere else. Just spread 'em and shut the fuck up — that way you're less bound to get beat up.

"Fuck you, you fuck!" Nadine yells back, her voice crackling and popping. She starts making toward the trailer but catches herself. What's she gonna do — burst in there and change the world? Fuck that! She turns around and heads in the other direction.

Eventually she comes to an oyster bed, so she follows it upstream. She comes to a shack surrounded by animal skulls. She walks up to the door and pounds on it like a cop.

"What?!" Mother Kralik screams from inside. "Hold your horses!"

Mother Kralik comes to the door and yanks it open. Her place stinks like rotten meat. Nadine pushes her way inside.

"You look like you could use a drink," Mother Kralik says, bemused.

"Yeah," Nadine says, "I'll have me one."

She sits down at the table where Mother Kralik has been constructing wax dolls. One of them is a sort of grotesque Barbie doll, with oversized boobs and yellow grass for hair.

Mother Kralik sits down across from Nadine and removes the doll, then pours two shots in some cups. She slides a shot toward Nadine, and Nadine immediately slams it. Mother Kralik pours another shot for Nadine. A bigger shot.

"How'd your date with the rich bitch go?" Mother Kralik asks, a smirk affixed to her face.

Nadine downs the next shot, then hesitates. Her voice is slurry when she speaks. Clean shirts appear in her head. "I'll kill that bitch! The fucking bitch, I'll fucking kill her!"

"Oh, come on now," Mother Kralik says, obviously trying to get her goat. "She means no harm to you. And it's not like she's any prettier than you."

Nadine stares at Mother Kralik in disbelief. How could that ugly old hag say a thing like that?

"What?!" Nadine snaps. "I can't believe you'd say such a thing! She's *way* prettier than me, she's sexier than me, and she's got everything I don't, including . . . including . . . including . . ."

"What?" Mother Kralik asks, pretending to inflect a maternal concern in her voice. "What does she got? Does she got a livelier personality than you? Does she got better clothes than you? Does she got more money than you? Is she taller than you, smarter than you, more worldly than you? Is she a better fuck than you?"

"You know what she's got!" Nadine returns, growing more and more enraged. "She's got everything! She's got this island by the balls! She's got Yann by the balls! She's even got you by the balls!"

Mother Kralik twists a wrist in her hand and pours Nadine an even bigger shot, grinning like a pedophile. "Now, now . . . she's a lovely, lovely girl," she tells Nadine. "She'll probably marry one of our men and have lovely little children with him."

Nadine flings her cup to the floor. It shatters. "Bullshit!" she shouts. "That's my department!"

Again, Mother Kralik feigns concern. "Oh, Nadine, you poor, poor thing. You must control your rage. This is what you do . . . When your hate boils over like that, you gotta keep it all inside. You gotta smother it, keep it down. Or else you'll end up, well, hurting yourself."

Looking at the ceramic shards all over the floor, Nadine is suddenly terrified. "Hurting myself?" she asks.

"Yes," Mother Kralik says, sipping her whiskey. "I didn't want to tell you, but I had a vision . . ."

"You saw something?"

Mother Kralik twists her wrists and glares across the table to let Nadine know she isn't fooling around. "Yes," she tells the foolish little twit, and pours her a new shot in another cup. "But remember, fate can be reversed if you want it to. You control your destiny, you control what happens. But you can blow it. So don't blow your top, or you'll lose sight of what you need to see. If you feel the barometer start to rise, you gotta force it back down. You gotta *not* go with it. Don't even scream. Crawl into bed and pull the covers up over your head, and wait."

Nadine guzzles her whiskey, buries her face in her hands, and tries to choke down the growls rising from inside. The words of the old witch carry a lot of truck with her. She's the one who yanked her into the world, as well as her mother, and most of the women on the island — and Mother Kralik hasn't let them forget it. She's also the one who won't let them forget that she has powers they don't have — which is why Nadine believes that Mother Kralik has been looking into her mind ever since she can remember.

Nadine's skin instantly goes clammy, and she feels a trickle of sweat drip from her pit. Should she apologize for that day in the cove?

"That's all right," Mother Kralik assures her and pours her a double. Nadine takes a glug and downs it all. She pours herself another shot.

"Let me give you some advice," Mother Kralik tells her. "It's okay to laugh. Just remember that! You can always laugh. Laughter is your only salvation."

Nadine nods to show she understands, then places a hand to her forehead. She wonders if she's feverish but knows she isn't *having* a fever. She *is* a fever.

Things start to swirl — she's got to get home! Nadine downs the rest of her drink, then staggers to her feet. The whole place reels.

"Are you all right?" Mother Kralik asks, feigning concern, but Nadine doesn't answer. She heads for the door.

"Are you sure you're all right?" Mother Kralik asks again, but Nadine ignores her. She blunders out into the night.

"Remember," Mother Kralik calls after her, "laughter is your only salvation!"

She watches Nadine swerve toward the beach and laughs at the little moron. She'll get what's coming to her. Oh yes, she'll get exactly what she deserves!

Nadine stumbles home without getting raped, falls into bed, and everything spins. That bitch! That bitch is fucking Yann right now! While she's preggy! And Yann doesn't love her! Cuz of that bitch, that bitch, *that fucking bitch!*

Nadine pulls the covers up over her head and growls like a fiend from hell. "Rrrrrrr! Rrrrrrr! Rrrrrrrrrr!" She holds it all in. She can't fall asleep. Hours go by, she stares at forms in the darkness. Maybe she's asleep and maybe she isn't. Maybe she's just dreaming she's awake. She can't tell. It's four in the morning. She's hot, she's sweaty, she's wet, she's horny. She's either fingering herself or dreaming she is. She's drunk and can't get off. She gets up — but still doesn't know if she's awake or not. She doesn't know shit.

Like a zombie, Nadine wanders out into the street. When she comes to April's house, she enters the yard and goes into the house. Then suddenly she's there, and so is April, lying in her bed. It's all a dream, it's gotta be a dream! How could it not be a dream?

Nadine pulls back the sheets, and there it is, her rich bitch nakedness, totally exposed, and lying there all succulent, with those monster tits beckoning her. And her snatch — dim in the dusk of the room. That body — she could either kill it or lick it to death.

April moans and places her hand on her own crotch. She's out of it, and rubbing it — still fucked up. She doesn't know Nadine is in the room. She doesn't know she's having a wet dream. She doesn't know anything.

Nadine places her hand beneath her own dress and feels

her crotch. Her panties are damp, and full, like a sack of pudding.

April moans again, still fiddling with her clit. She separates the folds in it. She wants it.

Slowly, gently, Nadine gets down on the bed and follows April's thighs up to her musk. The opening is slick and pungent, delicate and ready. Nadine touches her tongue to the nub and licks a briny bead.

"April," Nadine mutters, but she can't think of anything else to add — so says her name a few more times, even though she knows she sounds pathetic. "April . . . April . . ."

April moans again and squirms, lifting her legs just a bit. Nadine gets in there, burying her face in it. The softness of April's sex pulls her tongue in. Nadine delves as deep as she can, moves her tongue around, then goes to town, lapping like a terrier — doing to April what she would have her do to her. It doesn't matter who is getting serviced, it's happening to both of them. Nadine feels it rising inside her. She is in love and she's about to come. She can't help it, she starts to cry.

April, however, pulls Nadine's face in farther, thrusting her pelvis into her face. Nadine's sobs are stifled, she can hardly breathe — yet still, she is on the edge of coming as she licks away at April's clit, jiggling it — while April increases the grind in her groin.

And then April comes — or at least that's the way it seems to Nadine — who suddenly feels a smack against her ear. Maybe April meant to cuff her, maybe she didn't. Maybe that's not even what happened. Nadine can't tell, but that doesn't matter at the moment, because now she's starting to come herself. Flashes are flashing inside. Smack!

Smack! She pulls back, gasps, and feels her muscles jerking all over.

And still, she is crying. Crying because she's never felt this way before, crying because April let her lick her pussy — and there's no other place she would rather be than where she is, getting from April what nobody else has ever given Nadine in her entire life. Something she can't name but knows, because it hits her in the solar plexus — and she knows she will never get it again. Or feel this way again.

And so she bawls — in orgasm — as the flashes increase in her head. *Smack! Smack!* Blackness, whiteness, darkness, light. *Smack!* She's hot, she's cold — she can't even see. The smackings get harder. They're outside of her and inside too. *Smack! Smack! Smack!* Now it's not so comfortable.

Nadine rises and the flashes cease. She aims herself toward the door. She runs as fast as she can, away from April, away from her own mortification, assailing her wherever she blunders — laughing at her, mocking her: *"Haw haw haw haw!"* The laughter chases after her, across the beach, into the streets, and into the dusk of dawn.

In the morning Nadine is in her room, not knowing if she really went out or if she dreamt it all. All she knows is it feels like there's an infection coming on — no doubt from all that finger fucking of late. She's never jacked off so much in her life.

Nadine has a splitting headache. She rolls over and looks at the clock. Shit! She's late for work.

"Fucking fuck!" she mumbles, gets up, gets dressed, and

throws a couple aspirins down. Her mother is sitting at the kitchen table, just as late for work as she is.

"C'mon," Nadine says and leads her mom out the door. They walk down to the factory, and Nadine leaves her in the lobby. Someone will find her and put her to work — if what she does can really be called work.

Nadine walks up the street, trying not to blow chow. The day sucks. It's gray and dingy, like dirty bathwater, and she isn't quite clear about the night. She knows that April stole her man, and that her neck had gone berserk — so that's why she went out and got drunk. Probably down at the Dirty Dawgfish. Where else?

For some reason, though, Nadine is not pissed off. For some reason, she just feels indifferent, and she doesn't know why. For some reason, she also feels oddly . . . satiated.

And there's a phrase in her mind that keeps repeating: "Laughter is your only salvation . . . laughter is your only salvation . . . laughter is your only salvation."

Why is she saying this to herself? Did the Lord come and speak to her like to Joan of Arc? Yeah . . . that's gotta be it!

Nadine keeps heading up the hill, repeating this phrase in her mind. It will keep her sane. She will transcend.

"Laughter is your only salvation . . . laughter is your only salvation . . . Laughter is your only salvation . . . laughter is your only salvation . . . Laughter is your only salvation . . . laughter is your only salvation . . . Laughter is your only salvation . . . laughter is your only salvation . . . Laughter is your only salvation . . . laughter

is your only salvation . . . Laughter is your only salvation
. . . laughter is your only salvation . . . Laughter is your
only salvation . . . laughter is your only salvation . . . Laughter is your only salvation . . . laughter is your only salvation . . . Laughter is your only salvation . . . laughter is
your only salvation . . . Laughter is your only salvation . . .
laughter is your only salvation . . . Laughter is your only salvation . . .

Nadine reaches April's fence and wanders into the yard.
Yann, wearing another brand-new shirt, is sitting on the
porch with April. His duffel bag and accordion are at his
feet. They're eating breakfast. No doubt his dick is still
wet.

"Oh, good morning, Nadine," April says, her voice un-
usually flat.

"You look like shit," Nadine is surprised to hear herself
say.

But it's true. April doesn't have any makeup on, her hair
is in tangles, and there are circles beneath her eyes.

"You can say that again," April agrees. "I don't know
what happened last night . . . I have a splitting headache
and cottonmouth. I feel all drained. I think I got sick or
something."

"You did," Nadine tells her, "and it wasn't a pretty
sight."

"I can't remember much," April says, "but thanks to
Yann . . . I somehow made it to my bed."

"I bet you did," Nadine says.

She doesn't even look at Yann, and Yann tries not to look
at her.

"Well," April says, "I guess you could start by picking up the house. The place is a mess pretty much everywhere, especially the kitchen. Yann is not the tidiest cook, but it was so nice of him to come over and make breakfast for me. I'm sure I would've had to wait for you to come if it wasn't for him, because I can hardly lift a finger."

"Sure," Nadine says and clomps inside. Why would that rich bitch even tell her that crock a shit if she wasn't trying to cover something up?

Still, Nadine is surprised that seeing them together didn't make her blow her top. She's so surprised, in fact, that she laughs. A laugh she's never laughed before.

"Haw haw haw haw."

Outside, staring at their ham and eggs, Yann and April hear the laughter, and look up with uncertain expressions. It's a strange laugh — a laugh they've never heard before. And not a happy one.

But then it stops, so they chuckle to each other and go back to eating. Yann starts gobbling his breakfast down as April pokes her yolk. It pops, and an orange fluid oozes from it, spreading across her plate.

17

OWN AT THE DOCKS, One Eye and the captain are readying the boat to drag for sculpin, or bullheads as they're called on the island — which hosts a special breed: the Arctic cabezone, which spawn nowhere else in the world. It's the most Gothic of its kind, with unimaginable bubble eyes, a behemoth toad head, ornate fins, a greasy, oily hide, and a belly that bulges with other fish, which are also thrown into the mix and chopped up into dog food, no matter their state of decomposition. And this is how they're caught:

First the fishermen chum the kelp fields with what is left from the shark bombardment. Then the boats go out and drop their dredging nets — which is illegal in all countries of the world, because dredging drags across the bottom, tearing up ecosystems. Plants are uprooted, shellfish are disturbed. Dredging affects every single organism there, down to the microorganics. It takes decades to recover. An area is never the same. Fish take off, populations are lost, extinction occurs. All in the name of dog food.

The fishermen reason that this is recycling: using cod chum to bring on the shark, and shark chum to attract the sculpin, and sculpin chum to lure ratfish, and so on. But what they don't know is that chum works only when there are bottom feeders to entice. And every year there are fewer and fewer.

Modern Arctic cabezone are not the same as they were a century back. They have moved from the weeds to the rubble, where the nets can't reach. Where they no longer grow strong and fat but rather anemic — because of the scarcity of natural plants and therefore nutrition.

Which is why the diet of the Arctic cabezone has become completely different, now that they compete with rockfish and eels, and the other fish of the rubble — whose jaws are stronger, more conducive to crunching up crustaceans. Which is why Arctic cabezone are now stunted mutants, only half as large as they used to be.

This means that the Arctic cabezone, in essence, is gone from the planet, and has been replaced by a weaker species, with less efficient genes. Thanks to the fishermen of the island.

One Eye and the captain whistle as they work. Charlie and Lester and Fred come onboard, wheeling tubs of chum. All of them are sporting new shirts, and being careful not to spill.

"Morning, Gaston."

"Morning, Frederick. Nice day, eh?"

Greetings are exchanged all around. And then some tomfoolery:

"Hey, Cappy, since when did you start shaving?"

"Aww, lay off, Charlie! Since when did you start wearing deodorant?"

All the men laugh and go about their various chores. They all know when the change came about, but nobody is willing to admit it. They're fine with feeling fine. And not even angry at Yann for being late, and not helping out. He'll be along soon. They know it — and they envy him for this.

"Look at those hypocritical sonsabitches!" Mother Kralik scoffs, coming out of the cannery. It's cig break time, and the women are following her.

"Yeah!" Widow Flanahan puts in. "What the fuck's gotten into them?! With their snazzy new shirts and their spiffy little attitudes! Those fucking fucks!"

"You know damn well what's gotten into them!" Mother Kralik snaps. "They're outta their fucking minds! They're living in a dream-fucking-world! They think some angel is sitting on their face!"

"I sat on Charlie's face once," Widow O'Reilly puts in, "but the fucker never came back!"

"Why's that?" Mother Kralik asks. "Cuz you were old and fat and dripping like wax? Cuz you were starting to rot? Cuz there was some younger, sweeter pussy around, like your daughter?!"

Widow O'Reilly doesn't even have to answer. It's the same story for all of them. Nadine's mother, however, is in a bit better shape, standing there obliviously scratching her ass.

"Fuck them!" Widow Flanahan puts in. "Those fucking fuckers, they wanted it once! But once they stick it to you, they can't stand your childbearing hips and saggy tits! We can't help it! Fuck those fucks for fucking us!"

"Yeah!" Widow Flanahan adds. "Fuck those fucking fuckers! They fuck us and then we're trashed! Kaput! Forget it! And they don't change no fucking diapers! Nope! Go out and get drunk, that's what!"

"Come on, girls," Mother Kralik says, "let's go give them a piece of our mind!"

"Hey," One Eye says to the crew, "where the fudge is Yann?"

The fishermen crack up. They've never heard anyone substitute *fudge* for *fuck* before.

"I don't know," the captain answers, "maybe he's fudging on his fudging way."

Again the men guffaw. Being wholesome is inventive.

"Hey, assholes!" Mother Kralik says, walking up to the boat. Her hags are standing behind her, all of them covered with dogfish blood.

"Yes?" One Eye asks. "May I help you ladies?"

For a moment there is silence, then the men burst out in laughter, spraying saliva. They try to hold it in, but they can't. They laugh even harder. The idea of these old hags as *ladies* is laughable.

"Yeah!" Mother Kralik tells them. "You can tell us what the fuck's up with the shirts and shit! Is the Pope coming or something?!"

"Yeah!" Widow Flanahan adds. "Who you trying to impress?! April?! Shee–it! That bitch'd never have nothing to do with the likes of you . . . fucking One Eye, you fucking loser!"

"Ahem," One Eye answers her, pretending to clear his throat. "The name is Gaston. And as for your gracious opinion, it really doesn't matter to me. As you can see, we are busy —"

"Busy being full of shit!" Widow O'Reilly breaks in. "She ain't no angel! I mean, what the fuck. I mean, you think you're better than us or something?! Talking like gentlemen and shit? Combing your hair and shit? You ain't better than us! You're the fucking same as us! So cut the fucking shit!"

The other men get back to work, but One Eye feels the need to act as their ambassador.

"Madam," he bows, "I am deeply sorry if we offended your delicate sensibilities. It's just that we feel like being tidy, okay? Now there's no harm in that, is there?"

"Yes!" Mother Kralik says, pointing a bloodstained finger at him. "There's harm in you fuckers acting like you're the Shit! Cuz you ain't the Shit! You're just the same as us! You kill fish, we kill fish! We make dog food, you make dog food! And when somebody washes up on shore, dead or alive, you're just as guilty as we are when some schnauzer in the Ukraine takes a dump! Like that guy with the rings . . . you made him into dog food just as much as we did! We're all in on it, fucker! We're in the same goddamn fucking boat!"

"Maybe so," One Eye says, "but the difference between us and you is that you are covered in smelly blood, and we are wearing nice new shirts."

"Fuck you!" Widow Flanahan bursts out. "You limp-dick piece of shit!"

"And it feels nice to wear nice shirts," One Eye calmly goes on, "and exhibit some pride in personal hygiene. You should try it sometime. You might feel better about your-selves."

The fishermen snicker — and that's when the whistle at the factory blows, signaling the women to get back to work.

Mother Kralik decides to go for one last jab. "Nope!" she tells One Eye, "that's not the difference between you dickless fuckers and us! I'll tell you what the main differ-ence is! The main fucking difference is that you fucking want to fucking kiss that rich bitch's ass! Oh yes! You've got shit all over your nose already, *Gaston!* She ain't no saint, she's got a motherfucking asshole, so don't go pre-tending she's Mother Teresa! She sits on the shitter just like you. And her shit stinks! Just like yours . . . though probably not as bad! My point being, you fuckers want to rape her, because you want to rape your mommies, but you ain't got no mommies no more! All you got is us, we're your motherfucking mommies, and it's gross for you to have to rape us! So you want April for your mommy, because you're a fucking baby! You're all fucking babies! Hairy fucking fat stinking babies that want to rape their fucking mommies!"

One Eye rolls his eye toward the sky. "You think that makes an impression on us? You think that what comes out of your trash-mouth sounds like anything other than jeal-ousy? Haw! You're just an ugly old hag who never got a chance to bloom. You're jealous, all of you! Because *we* ad-mire beauty."

"You're *rapists!*" Widow O'Reilly shouts out. "So don't pretend you ain't! Raping your daughters, raping your wives, dreaming of raping April! Rapists! All of you!"

"Say your little theory does hold water," One Eye replies. "Say we do want to 'rape April,' as you so crudely put it . . . then what's the difference? I mean, is what you want to do to her so different than what you accuse us of? As if what you would do isn't as horrible as what we would do — if your little theory is true. And maybe it is and maybe it isn't. But regardless if it is or isn't, you'd do worse and you know it!"

The whistle blows again. Mother Kralik, however, refuses to budge. She has locked eyes with One Eye and is glaring into his brain. He pretends her scowl doesn't touch him, as his statement hangs in the air about the women — and they all know it's true: they'd use torture and mutilation, they'd destroy completely — to destroy what's been destroyed in themselves. An eye for an eye, a cunt for a cunt!

Mother Kralik starts to mumble and roll her eyes around in her head. The way her body starts to jerk, it looks as if she's being poked by invisible pins.

"Uh oh," Widow O'Reilly utters.

"Oh shit," Widow Flanahan says.

"Curse ye!" Mother Kralik suddenly snaps, her voice rising from an unfamiliar place in the bottom of her thorax. Her eyes are nowhere to be seen. *"For now I cast my curse upon thee! At sea! You're fucked, mister!"*

One Eye stares back, nonchalantly. He doesn't respond. The whistle blows again as Mother Kralik's eyes pop back. And then the women turn and go.

Charlie and Lester walk up to One Eye. He's standing

there like a mannequin, as if his feet are pinned to the deck. He's staring at the hags walking away.

"Come on," Lester says, slapping him on the back, "don't worry about that."

"Yeah," Charlie adds, "don't worry, be happy."

One Eye turns toward them and forces a smile. "Crazy old loon," he eventually says. His words seem as forced as his grin. "She can't do nothing . . . she's full of it." Still, he doesn't look too convinced.

"Where's that Yann?" the captain asks, coming up from the hold. "We're ready to head out."

One Eye breaks from his daze. "Yann!" he answers, pretending cheer. "Yeah! Where is that guy?! I s'pose we better sound the foghorn."

"Okay," Fred says. He goes to the cabin and pulls the cord, blasting the horn. The men begin untying the boat. They'll give him a few minutes, the lucky bastard.

18

NADINE WALKS INTO THE KITCHEN but doesn't feel much like doing dishes. She decides to start picking up the house from the top down, so she walks up the stairs and into April's room. The place is a mess, just like she envisioned it: clothes all over the floor, the bed unmade — and in the center of it a giant wet spot.

Nadine starts to see red again, and her impulse is to let out a scream — but then she hears that voice in her head ("Laughter is your only salvation . . .") so restrains herself. And it makes her feel powerful to hold it in.

Nadine laughs and strips the bed. She knows that laughter is a cover-up, and it hides the way she really feels — she knows that if she doesn't laugh, then she doesn't deny. And if she doesn't deny, then the truth is right there in her face, and that could be deadly.

Nadine laughs again. She decides to spy on April and Yann. She sneaks downstairs and tiptoes to the window by the porch. Through the curtains, they can't see her but she can see them.

"I must admit," April says, "it did take a couple cups of coffee to get me going this morning. But I feel much better now."

Nadine recognizes April's nonstop tone returning. She's starting to blabber again, as always.

"Well," Yann tells her, "I'll be sailing out today."

"Sailing!" she teases him. "You call yourself a sailor? Where've you been, Anchorage? Homer? Juneau? That's what I thought. Some sailor you are. I'm more of a sailor than you, ya know. Let's see . . . the Mediterranean, Italy, Greece, the South of France . . . around the Cape, Tahiti, Hawaii, the world! I've sailed the world, Yann, I've done it all! Well, actually, that's not true — but I'm still more of a sailor than you. Once I even sailed to —"

That blabbering bitch, Nadine thinks. She can see Yann leaning forward, intent on every word she says.

"— Ecuador! I'm not kidding, Yann, a person can sail around the planet! And if you're going to call yourself a sailor, then you should sail more than just down to King Salmon. You should definitely do some sailing in tropical climates. A foxy hunk like you could take his pick in Tahiti. The men, of course, are just as beautiful as the women, but the women, they'd flip for you, Yann! You could have the island princess! No, you could have two of them!"

April stops talking for a nanosecond and stabs the last piece of egg on her plate. But Yann is hypnotized and doesn't even know she isn't talking until he sees the egg slip between her lips — those lips that are going up and down for him, opening and closing for him, puckering for him, forming syllables for him . . .

"Look, Yann," April says, with a slightly serious tone,

"next time you're out there sailing around for the halibut —
ha ha — just ask yourself, *What the hey?* Then start making
for Tahiti. Or the Caribbean! Anywhere. Just don't *not* do
it, or you'll end up never doing it, and the consequence of
that is that you won't get to open up your world. So open
up your world, Yann, sail the world! Tahitian maidens!
Take it from me, Yann, I'm a writer, and writers know
these things."

April has a little bit of yolk on her lower lip. Yann has
been watching it. Her tongue flashes for just a second. It
searches out the drop, darts at it, licks it off, and then it's
gone. Unknowingly, Yann imitates her tongue with his,
licking at the same exact spot on his lip.

"But Hawaii," April goes on, pouring herself another
cup of coffee, "Hawaii's the place! That is, if you can afford
it. A starving writer and a dirt-poor fisherman, of course,
would have trouble affording anything in Hawaii, much
less the boat to sail there on. But I've got resources, Yann.
If you ever want to take a jaunt down there, just let me
know. I'm talking grass skirts, native sun, slinky bikinis,
Hawaiian dances . . . this is how they dance, Yann. The
hula! Beautiful girls. Beautiful, beautiful, beautiful girls!"

April jumps up and starts swinging her rump. Yann's
eyes, however, are affixed to her lips.

"What do you write?" he asks. "Novels?"

"Well," April says, sitting back down, "I haven't really
written anything yet, but that's because I'm waiting for the
right time. It might even be in the middle of the night.
When a writer gets hit by an idea, it doesn't matter what
time of day it is, she's got to get it down on paper! So, when
the idea hits, I don't care what I'm doing, I'm going to stop

everything and get it, and take it from there. I'll probably write about my life."

"Your life?" Yann asks. "Sailing around?"

"Well, some of it would be about that, but some of it would be about other stuff. You know, the people I know, the places I've been, the jobs I've done —"

"What jobs?" Yann asks.

"Well . . ." April says, not so sure she wants to bring this up, "you know, various things here and there, mostly in California. I've actually led quite a life. It would surprise you, Yann."

Nadine pictures April's life back on the mainland: she gets up in the morning and the butler brings her breakfast on the veranda while the maid goes upstairs and cleans the sheets she's been getting fucked on. Then a truckload of money comes in, freshly made off the exploitation of poor people, and April directs it to one of her private vaults. The truck pulls up and a giant vacuum cleaner sucks thousands of dollars out.

Nadine can't help it, she laughs at her own imagination. *"Haw haw haw haw."*

Yann and April are taken by surprise to hear Nadine so close by. It's that laughter again — that disturbed, eerie laughter.

Nadine figures it's time to sneak away. So she slinks back upstairs, missing the final scene: Yann, a bit wigged out, stands up and bids April adieu, but she grabs him and hugs him before he walks off. "It was so sweet of you to come by this morning," she tells him, "and check on me. Be sure to stop by when you get back."

"I will," Yann says, "and don't booze it up too much."

April laughs and slaps him on the butt. He picks up his gear and starts making for the gate.

"And keep your eye out for a boat that can make it to Hawaii," she calls to him, "and catch lots of fish, Yann!"

"Okay," he calls back, then waves and steps out into the street. A foghorn can be heard sounding in the bay. It's telling him to get his ass onboard.

April watches him run down the hill, his tight-ass buns pumping away. Yeah, she thinks, and considers heading up to her room to jack off. But for some reason she doesn't feel the need — probably because of that wet dream she had in the night. She can't remember exactly what happened, but she knows it was good.

Yann runs for the dock and makes it to the boat right when it is pulling away. He leaps for it and lands on the deck. One Eye looks up. He actually has his hair combed.

"Where've ya been!" One Eye demands. "Romancing our new national treasure?"

Yann doesn't say anything, just smiles. It's nice to hear One Eye not saying *fucking this* and *fucking that*, it's nice to see the fishermen with clean new shirts, and an air of respect for themselves. And all because of April, because she landed on the island.

Yann heads for the bow and watches the shore pull away from the boat. Was she serious about going to Hawaii? And what, really, are her "resources"?

"She sure is something, ain't she?" One Eye asks, coming up and ribbing him. "Yessirree, St. April, that's what we should call her, closest thing to God ever landed on this rock. So holy she don't even shit."

Yann laughs. One Eye still has some of his old sense of humor left, as do the other fishermen.

"Hey!" the captain barks, coming around from the stern. "Who's got the crank?!"

"Who's got the whiskey?!" One Eye returns.

"Who's got the porno?!" Charlie shouts out.

"Right here!" Lester answers back. "I bought a box off Bubba's daughter! He won't be needing these anymore."

Yann goes to the rail and stares out to sea. It's a gorgeous day to envision April's lips.

"Holy fucking shit!" he suddenly hears One Eye exclaim. "Look at the stinking hooters on this bitch! Wait a second . . ."

There's something in his voice that makes Yann spin around — and when he does, he finds himself staring straight into the asshole of a centerfold gal. She's bending over and looking at the camera from between her legs, two great boobs dangling like udders — and an inviting look on her face like she likes to get it from behind. From anyone.

Yann, of course, looks for the bush. And there it is, beneath her ass, above her boobs, spread by a pair of parting fingers, revealing something erectile and pink, and slippery enough to slide right in.

"Whatta ya think?" One Eye asks.

"Whatta ya mean what do I think?" Yann answers back. "It's porn."

One Eye, however, doesn't have to tell Yann to look any closer, it's obvious who it is — back behind the flesh and the sex. But still, Yann searches for the face. And there it is. Everything changes.

One Eye lowers the porno mag, replacing April's face with his own. He's wearing an eager grin. "Looks like she does take a shit!" He laughs. "Haw haw haw!"

Yann is dumbstruck. He grabs the porno out of One Eye's hands and turns to the cover. It's a *Hustler,* and April's on the cover, sporting pasties on her knockers. "Million-Dollar Movie Muffs!" reads the caption. "See April Berger's T & A and Much Much More!"

"No way!" Yann says in disbelief. "No way in heck!"

The fishermen laugh at Yann.

"You better believe it!" One Eye shouts out. "She's a movie bitch and she's butt-ass naked! That's what she is! Bitch thinks she's better than us, the cunt! Hey, Yann, can you get me a piece, that is, if she ain't a fucking dyke?!"

Yann turns away, but the fishermen surround him, peering over his shoulders.

"Lemme see that slut-ass bitch!"

"Hey, man, that's my twat mag! Give it back!"

"C'mon, Yann! Stop hogging all the pussy!"

"Go away," Yann tells them, but of course they won't. Yann finds the section on April, and the sailors cheer and jeer with every picture of her.

"I wonder if that camera fucker got to stick it in her!" One Eye yucks. "Bitch'll fuck anything! Even me! Baw haw haw!"

"Shut up!" Yann orders him, paging through the never-ending beaver shots, looking for an explanation, as the fishermen, behind him, continue to roar with laughter. If they don't shut up, Yann thinks, he might have to teach somebody a lesson.

19

HALF A WEEK LATER, it's a menacing night of thunderheads, but as yet no rain has fallen on the island. Just heavy spring wind, and deep low rumbling sounds. The pressure is building.

In the thick tobacco haze of the Dirty Dawgfish, Yann is sitting with the men and Nadine is sitting with the women. Almost the entire island labor force is there, and everyone is getting drunk to celebrate St. Ratfish Eve. It's the night that signals the advent of the ratfish spawning season, when the men go out and drag for tons of slimy bubble-eyed ratfish bulging with roe. Then, when the men come back with their bilges full, it's customary for the women to greet them with a parade, in which a ratfish effigy is pelted with stones and garbage. It's the only holiday on the island besides Christmas.

The locals, dressed in dirty shirts, are guffawing and drinking hard. Those who do not drink to inebriation are chastised — even though this group is limited to one: Yann. He is sitting at a table with One Eye and the members of his crew, who are laughing uproariously over the uncovering of April.

"Let's hear it for the biggest whore around!" Mother Kralik screeches across the bar, standing on her chair. A thunderous communal cheer erupts. News travels fast on the island.

"Here's to our own candy-assed movie bitch!" One Eye puts in, raising his own mug of Bud.

The islanders love it. They stamp their feet and shout things out.

"No cunt-slut chippie is better than us!" Widow Flanahan screams and raises the centerfold for all to see. A hole has been gouged in the spot where April's vagina used to be. The bar bursts out in hilarious laughter.

"She's looking for a gang bang!" Charlie yells.

"Only a horse's cock could fill that skanky hole!" Widow O'Reilly adds.

"Maybe she's big news to the rest of the world!" Nadine joins in. "But to us she ain't nothing but a piece-of-shit bag of shit attached to a rotten pussy and a pair of fat-ass tits!"

The whole crowd, even Hans the bartender, roars with approval. Yann, however, is the exception, sinking lower and lower toward his beer. The only reason he's not with April is because the town would give him too much shit — but now it looks like that doesn't matter. They're giving him too much shit anyway.

"How about that Yann?" One Eye howls, elbowing Yann in the side. "Is that why you're her little flower boy?! Is that why you did all that work on her yard?! To get a piece of stinking tuna?!"

Yann ignores them all. He feels like crap as it is, and is hardly able to deal with the image of her he now holds in his head. He never even considered those parts of her body before, but now, that's all he can see: Vagina and butthole! Vagina and butthole! Vagina and butthole! . . . And it twists his guts to see her that way, looking at the camera that way — with a look on her face like she'd love it from anyone with a stiffie. Even a gorilla! Or One Eye!

But on top of that there's something else. It's the fact that April is a celebrity and none of them even knew it — which makes him feel like just another ignorant island slob, a fishing hick who doesn't know jack about what is going on in the world. A complete bozo!

Yann had been back on the island for a day, and had tried to work up the courage to visit her, but he just couldn't muster it. He didn't think he could look at her the same way anymore. Besides, even if he was able to get beyond these issues — which he knows he can — he'd get so much shit from the islanders that it wouldn't be worth it to be cast out by his kind.

Yann is scared — not to be a part of the place he's grown up in, scared to leave those he's been saving up money to flee. Before, Northern California was a dream — but now, the idea of actually severing his ties is becoming a reality. He'd lose his job, his island, his fish. He'd lose his people, even if they are a bunch of assholes. He needs time to think.

And what could April possibly want from him? He's just a run-of-the-mill dime-a-dozen fisherman, whereas she's a star — who has bared it all. But why?! Because she's a slut?

And then there's Nadine, across the room, constantly trying to catch his eye. He's been doing his best to avoid her, but he knows the worst is about to come. She will hold him to his promise — especially if she does have a bun in the oven. And then life will totally suck.

Yann grits his teeth and lowers his head. There isn't much he can do. If he leaves right now and goes to April, he'll basically be saying "Fuck you" to his people, and there will be consequences. It'd be better to take their abuse . . . for April's sake.

Yann peers at Nadine through the haze. She is as drunk as a skunk, occasionally rising to shout out stuff about April. Her expression curdles something in him. The fact that she would scream these things, then go back and work for her, wrenches his stomach even more. It can only mean trouble.

"She's a goddamned flea-bit shit-ass hooker!" Nadine shouts, her neck twisting, her crotch burning. Her PMS is kicking in, her infection has worsened, and she feels like a complete and utter bitch.

"I'm telling you," Mother Kralik adds, addressing the patrons of the Dirty Dawgfish, "she'll be the ruin of us all! She's writing a book, folks! Gee, I wonder what it could be about! It'll probably be a best-seller, and then we'll all be laughing stocks!"

A different noise begins to rise. It's a murmur of assent, similar to those muttered back in German taverns, circa 1932. Mother Kralik is changing the mood of the crowd. Now they're starting to actually think, even if their thinking is distorted.

Nadine looks at her mother, smoking away on a cig. There's a two-inch cake of ash attached to her butt, and she's smoking the filter.

"And then it'll be a movie, no doubt!" Mother Kralik continues. "Because movie bitches got movie contracts! And what do you think that movie'll be about?! A bunch of scummy fishermen?! A bunch of scummy factory whores?! Or all of the above?!"

The murmurs increase and the tumult builds. Beer swills, whiskey gurgles. To anybody from anywhere else, it would appear a carnival of drunken misfits, roaring boors, flying spittle, gnashing maws, and guttural cries spewing forth like public defecations.

Which is exactly what April witnesses as she opens the door and looks into the bar. For a second she thinks it's her imagination, as logic informs her that such a bestiary could only exist in the imagination of some sicko — because what she sees is a mass of frothing jackals and hyenas howling at her, pointing at her, and launching their indecipherable on-slaught on her, all of them competing to be heard — their turgid taunts and squalid squeals exploding from a hell of horrid gorges.

April immediately slams the door upon this scene — this scene she knows is opposed to her, like a bedlam bent on her destruction — like some sort of nightmare rendered by Bosch, too surreal to be real. She begins heading up the street, livid, knees shaking. Somewhere in the yellow smoke, she'd seen Nadine screeching at her.

But was that really what she'd seen? Or was it all just paranoia? Her skin crawls all over her body. She shivers.

All she wanted to do was find Yann, who she knew was back on the island. She couldn't understand why he hadn't come to visit her, so she'd gone down to find him — only to find that godawful apocalypse of souls condemned to living admist their own shit — like baboons at the zoo smearing themselves with excrement. Because life doesn't matter, and death doesn't matter, when it's the same four walls every day, and the same empty eyes every day, and the same piles of shit every day. Festering festering every day . . .

This is the analogy April comes up with. And she can't help thinking this, since the expressions on the faces she just saw were as hateful as those in the zoo her parents used to take her to. In the monkey house when she was a kid — back when an irate primate had flung monkey shit at her for looking at him as if he was a lower-level life form than she. April shivers again.

She needs to see Yann. Over the last couple of days, she had gone through a pack of batteries. The thought had crossed her mind that maybe Nadine had discovered her secret and had indulged herself as well, but she instantly rejected this. Nadine had been a loyal maid. That couldn't 've been her in the bar!

April trembles and increases her stride, heading home to Bun-bun and Elphy and her book she can't write. She's no writer and she knows it! She has no ear for placing syllables next to each other; she thinks Jewel is a poet.

Maybe she shouldn't have told Nadine she was writing a book. Maybe that was why they reacted that way — because they don't take kindly to writers. Or had they discovered who she really is?

There is no way to tell. April jumps up her steps, swings the door open, steps in, and bolts the dead bolt behind her — which is something she has never done on the island before.

Meanwhile, down at the Dirty Dawgfish, One Eye is teasing Yann: "Haw haw! How about that, Yann?! She went running out looking for a bigger dick! Cuz that's all she is! A crab-bit stink-ass whore with a grubby stretched-out pussy! A pus cunt, that's what! She's a cocksucking shit-licking Hollywood bimbo! And I'm gonna fuck her in her turd-hole, that's what I'm gonna do! Whatta ya say, fellas, shall we go pay the little lady a visit?!"

Yann snaps. It's like watching somebody else, but he knows it's him. It's him jumping up and grabbing One Eye by the neck. It's him shoving One Eye against the wall, intent on bashing his skull into splinters. It's him getting ready to throw all his weight into his fist, which is aiming at the center of One Eye's pathetic face, soon to be pulp. His head'll hit the wall and break open like a pumpkin. Brains will splatter all over the place. Yann knows it, he sees it. It's gonna happen! By God!

But he can't pull the trigger — to release the tension in the spring. He's holding back — waiting for something. But what? For One Eye to yell out and die like a coward? For the crowd to push him over the edge? For someone to stop him?

"Come on!" someone yaps.

"Kill the bastard!" another voice barks.

"Finish the motherfucker off!" somebody howls.

Yann can't even see; he's in a blind rage. It all happens in a whirling blur. Yann fights it, even though it's telling him to smash the skull into the wall, to transform evil into gore. He's a millimeter from losing it. But if the spring springs, he knows he'll be that guy! That guy who lost it! And he will not be that guy! Let it be somebody else!

Yann's sight returns, and he sees a single bulging eye, staring back at him. One Eye has just seen the end of himself in Yann's fogged vision, and it was enough to make him drop a load in his pants.

"Hey, look!" somebody yells, pointing down at One Eye's boot. "Old One Eye's gotta case of the Hershey squirts!"

The smell rises, shocking Yann completely back. He releases the windpipe in his grip and drops the body to the floor. Nobody says anything, and Yann looks around. Now they know how far they can push him. Now they know what will happen to them if they mess with April.

Yann heads toward the door, opens it, and walks out. He is no longer part of the clan.

Nadine feels her neck twitch again. She hates that fucker. She hates him, she hates him, *She hates him,* SHE HATES HIM! It should've been her honor he defended — not that porn slut's, Goddammit!

"Well, well, well," Mother Kralik says, twisting her wrists and turning toward Nadine. "Looks like you've got a demon in you, eh?"

Nadine does not respond. Mother Kralik goes on. "What's wrong, honey, can't you even control your own neck? Don't you have any control at all? Have you given in?"

Nadine still won't respond. Her neck continues to twitch.

"Or is this the way you really are?" Mother Kralik goads her on. "Is this your natural state? Have you come back to who you truly are? Because everyone knows, you weren't anybody before! Nope, just a silly little whore who got it in the ass from her daddy! Whose mother left her! Whose future is the factory, dried-out tits, and a useless cunt! Who doesn't have nothing except what she makes up! Is that who you are?"

Nadine turns toward Mother Kralik, her neck twitching even faster. Still, there's a calm on Nadine's face that is impressive to the hag.

"But what can you do?" Mother Kralik asks, lighting a cig. "You can't do nothing. You're stuck. You're trapped. Trapped in your own head, in a body that won't stop quaking like a goddamned vibrator. You're a powerless little bitch, that's what you are. There's nothing in the world you can do. Unless, that is, doing something about it is more important to you than the world — your world, your empty world of make-believe fathers you re-create into lovers, who won't even have you! But don't worry, dear, you still have me. Oh yes. You can always count on me. I'm here for ya honey."

"Haw haw haw haw haw!" Nadine responds, laughing right in Mother Kralik's face, laughing that hellacious laughter — *"Haw haw haw haw haw haw haw!"* — as Mother Kralik pretends to cower, as the widows look on agog.

"Haw haw haw haw haw!" Nadine laughs the laughter of the damned.

20

NADINE STEPS OUT and into the thunder, clutching at her neck, and then her head. Her neck is twitching as usual, but her head is doing something new. It's flashing with white light. She grips her skull even harder, trying to contain the force within. It's no use. She looks up at the cocksucking sky.

Black clouds flash with electric yellow veins. The storm broods, smothering the light. Nadine tries to laugh but can't. What emerges is a menacing rumble. *"Rrrrrrrrr!"* she growls, then takes off up the street, tweeking all over like she's going cold turkey.

When she gets to her trailer, she goes bursting in and heads for the shitter. She stares transfixed at her neck in the mirror, twitching away with a mind of its own. For a second she considers severing some cords but then decides to save her rage.

"Fucking stop it!" she yells at herself, then tears off her clothes as if they were paper. She stands before her naked self, staring at the stranger in the mirror. She has never seen this woman in her life: dark furrowed brow, teeth bared carnivorously; neck yanking and yanking and yanking at her chest.

"Stop it!" Nadine screams. "Fucking stop it!" But she won't.

She stomps into her room and jumps into bed, pulling the covers over her head. She grips her knees and pulls herself into a small, tight ball, trying to hold the violence in.

"Rrrrrrrrr!" she growls, trying not to scream. She hates everything. If there was a big red button in front of her that said ANNIHILATION OF EVERYTHING, she would jump up and push it.

Nadine tries to fall asleep but can't. The quaking eventually subsides, but the growling doesn't. Even when she starts drifing in and out of limbo, she is still rumbling like the darkness around her.

"Rrrrrrrr! . . . Rrrrrrrrr! . . . Rrrrrrrrr!"

Visions cycle through her head. Yann and April are fucking. She and Yann are fucking. She and April are fucking. The same three visions all night long. It's impossible to break from their monotony — it's driving her nutzoid. She's awake, she's asleep — it doesn't fucking matter. Wherever she is, it's always the same: April, Yann, her — fucking! Fucking Fucking Fucking Fucking!

"Rrrrrrrrrrrrrrrrrrrrrrrrrrrrrrrrrrrrrrrrrrrrrrrrrrrrrrr!!!"

The visions continue — all of them getting it in the ass.

By dawn Nadine is as strung out as the sky. She can't take another second, so she jumps out of bed and blunders into the kitchen. Her mother is sitting there, but Nadine doesn't give a ratfish's ass. She bumps into things, knocks stuff over, and makes it to the door. She throws it open and steps into the shittiness.

The sky is like a pile of shit, the earth is a giant diaper. She opens up her mouth to scream, but something holds her voice inside.

What?! What the fuck is holding her voice back? Nadine tries to let it out. She can't. It's like something is stifling her, choking her throat from inside. She opens her mouth as wide as it will go. She strains, eyes popping from their sockets. Nothing comes out.

A neighbor looks out and sees Nadine standing naked in the gloom, her mouth open like that of a gawking baby bird. Her body is shaking, she seems to be screaming — but there is no noise at all. Has she gone bonkers like her mother? That's what happens when no father is around! Look at that big ugly furry thing, all the way up to her navel! She should really trim it!

Nadine's eyes are rimmed in red and inflated to the size of golf balls. Her hair is a medusa of tangles and snarls, and the sky is a big dry nipple starving her to death. It isn't giving her shit! Nothing is giving her shit! She ain't got shit! Except *shit!*

Fucking sky! Piece-of-crud cunt-dripping sky! Goddamn yeast-infection rape-baby sky! Maggot-pussy cornhole sky! Vomit-reeking turd-queefing sky! Butt-fisting gerbil-felching Shit-ass sky! Sky of shmegma and piss! Sky of anal leakage! Sky of AIDS and VD and blackheads and hemorrhoids! Sky of abortion, cancer, and rancid Tampons! Sky of dick cheese, fecal matter, cocks and pricks and zits and tits! Sky of faggots, fuckheads, farts and phlegm!

Jew sky, Nigger sky, Spic sky, Chink sky, Honkie sky, Wop sky, sky of motherfucking everyone! SCUM-SUCKING OPEN-SORE DIARRHEA SKY!

Nadine leaps at it, claws at it. It laughs at her. She can't sink her claws into it. She can't do shit to it.

But she can sink her nails into herself! Nadine claws her face as the neighbor lady bolts her door. The sky contains its rumbling roar. Blood seeps out of Nadine's face. Haw! She has beaten the arrogant sky! The sky can't do *fucking fuck!* She is showing it, she is showing the world! Every time she tears at her face, every time she rends her flesh. Take that, Sky! Take that, you SONUVABOWLEG-GEDMENOPAUSEWHORE!!!

She laughs — she laughs that laugh again. Standing naked, sweat-soaked and quivering, blood streaming off her cheeks — laughing at the sky. But laughing in a different way, a new way, a way that has nothing to do with her own designs. It's got her, and it does what it wants. It has its own desire, she is merely serving it. Nadine is just a vessel of flesh, a sack of barf and piss and shit. Laughter lives inside her.

Nadine turns and goes back in. Her mother is sitting there expecting something, though she doesn't know what it is. There's a routine, that's all she knows. She wakes up and is taken to a place where she sits — though she doesn't even know who it is that takes her there. All she knows is that she goes where she is taken. And that the person who takes her there is standing there buck naked, and laughing at her, covered with blood and shaking like a psycho.

"*Haw!* Look at you!" Nadine screams at her mother.

"You're insane! Completely insane! *Haw! Haw haw haw haw!*"

Widow Murphy wants a cig. Some stupid kid is getting in her face, making her nervous. Every day she burns the food. Every day their silence gets louder. Their hatred thickens, boils, builds. Every fucking day. Will she get smacked? Probably . . .

Smack! Nadine lets her mother have it. Her mother goes flying to the floor, then gets up holding her stinging face. They burn their murderous glares at each other. There are knives in the kitchen and blades in their eyes — but nobody goes for the steel. They just stand there and stab each other with the fury of their pupils. Bitch! Whore! Slut! *Die!*

DIE! DIE! DIE! DIE!

DIE! DIE!

DIE!

21

EANWHILE, BACK AT THE CANNERY, Mother
Kralik brings the cleaver down, severing the
head of a rockfish off. *Whack!* She is stationed
along the decap belt. Every time a rockfish passes by, she
does her job.

WHACK! WHACK!

Something is in the air, the lights dim and surge, playing
tricks with violet fluorescence. Where the hell is Widow
Murphy?! Where the hell is Nadine?! Probably wiping that
rich bitch's ass. WHACK! Or scrubbing her unnatural tits!
WHACK! Or perfuming her celebrity cunt! WHACK!
WHACK! WHACK!

All the women whack away — even if they are not de-
heading fish. It's the motion of the day, sharp and erratic:
pulling levers, mopping guts, labeling cans. WHACK!
WHACK WHACK WHACK! everywhere. The factory
*whack*s away.

WHACK WHACK WHACK! WHACK WHACK
WHACK! WHACK WHACK WHACK WHACK

WHACK WHACK WHACK! WHACK WHACK! The
women glaring at each other. WHACK WHACK
WHACK WHACK WHACK WHACK WHACK
WHACK WHACK! WHACK WHACK WHACK
WHACK WHACK WHACK WHACK WHACK
WHACK WHACK WHACK WHACK WHACK!
Some bitch should die. WHACK WHACK WHACK
WHACK WHACK WHACK WHACK WHACK
WHACK WHACK WHACK WHACK WHACK
WHACK WHACK WHACK! Everyone would feel a
whole lot better. WHACK WHACK WHACK WHACK
WHACK WHACK WHACK WHACK WHACK
WHACK WHACK WHACK WHACK WHACK!
WHACK WHACK WHACK WHACK WHACK
WHACK WHACK WHACK WHACK! Jaws are tight,
eyes dart all over the place.
  WHACK WHACK WHACK WHACK WHACK
WHACK WHACK WHACK WHACK WHACK!
WHACK WHACK WHACK WHACK WHACK
WHACK WHACK WHACK WHACK WHACK
WHACK WHACK WHACK WHACK WHACK
WHACK WHACK WHACK WHACK WHACK
WHACK WHACK! WHACK WHACK WHACK
WHACK WHACK WHACK WHACK WHACK
WHACK WHACK WHACK WHACK WHACK
WHACK WHACK WHACK WHACK WHACK
WHACK WHACK WHACK! WHACK WHACK
WHACK WHACK WHACK WHACK WHACK
WHACK WHACK WHACK WHACK! WHACK
WHACK WHACK WHACK WHACK WHACK

It's as if the women are straining together. WHACK WHACK WHACK WHACK WHACK! Trying to make something happen together. WHACK WHACK WHACK WHACK WHACK WHACK WHACK WHACK! To break the weakest link in the chain. WHACK WHACK WHACK! Everyone's on edge. WHACK WHACK WHACK WHACK WHACK WHACK WHACK WHACK WHACK WHACK WHACK! Sixty percent are menstruating. WHACK WHACK WHACK WHACK WHACK WHACK WHACK WHACK WHACK WHACK WHACK WHACK WHACK WHACK WHACK WHACK WHACK WHACK WHACK! The lights flicker, the fish waver. WHACK WHACK! WHACK WHACK WHACK WHACK! WHACK WHACK WHACK WHACK WHACK WHACK WHACK! . . .

Somebody gives. The lights dim. All Mother Kralick sees are a flash of limbs. Somebody's running, flailing between the machines. Women screech with glee. A body passes like a blur.

"Slaughter her!" someone screams. "Slaughter the fat fucking squaw!"

It's some Native American bitch, one of the few on the island — and Mother Kralik is glad. Their race is disposable — who needs 'em? She's running too fast. *Splap!* Oil and steel halt her flight — a sanguine splatter rains through the place, spraying the women. Their screeches of delight increase in direct proportion to the amount of blood they're covered with.

Mother Kralik twists her wrists. A rockfish passes by and doesn't get the ax. Mother Kralik laughs. It's the same laugh Nadine is laughing half a mile away.

Winners kill, losers die.

22

YANN ET AL. come back with ratfish. It was a shitty
catch in shitty weather, and things had been shitty
at sea. The captain's allegiance had been with One
Eye, and so had the crew's. Nobody would talk to Yann,
and Yann had been forced to work by himself, mostly on
the shittiest jobs — like pumping out the bilge. He was being punished, of course, for stepping out of bounds.
There's a pecking order on the island, and he had disturbed it.

Luckily for Yann, he had been on good terms with the
crew for years. They had fished with him, and drank with
him, and listened to his music. They didn't want to treat
him like shit, but according to the norms of the island, they
had to. If it had been anyone else, he would've been beaten
to a pulp, or at least pissed on in the bilge.

Yann looks up and sees them milling around like convicts
in a prison yard. Occasionally, somebody spits into the hold.
This is not how he wanted to spend St. Ratfish Day —
which had always been his favorite day on the island.

St. Ratfish Day is the only day that children are allowed to strike back. As a kid, Yann used to run with the pack, smacking at some mystery adult dressed up as a ratfish. Usually they used sticks, or else they threw garbage. Now, however, Yann is too old for that.

Yann started fishing at the age of fifteen, to help his mother bring home the bacon. All his father ever did was sit around the house getting drunk, cleaning his gun, and sweating like a pig. Yann always thought his father sweated more than the average man.

Ever since his father stopped sweating, though, Yann had been on his own, and had lived like a miser. His home was a one-room trailer, one of those silver jobs that someone towed over back when there was a ferry. There was a hot plate in there, and a toaster, but not much more. It was lonely.

After the Big Run, Yann planned on taking his pay and leaving the island. There was no reason to stay. Especially if Nadine was going to have his kid.

"Ugh . . ." Yann groans and shakes his head at a ratfish. He has no qualms about making it splitsville on that scene. It doesn't matter to him if the kid is part his — the fact that it is Nadine's means it is doomed. And he will be too, if he tries to stay and make it work. She's nutso. Which is why he's on the next boat heading to Seattle. After the Big Run, that is.

Yann repositions the pump hose and shivers in the clammy darkness. There are ratfish all around him, but not as many as in years before. No doubt the mass capture of this species as it spawns, year after year after year after year, has cut down on the population around the island.

Yann looks at a ratfish but sees something different. What he sees are lips. April's lips. It's the first time he's seen them in days, and he's glad to see them again. They'd been missing from his illusionary world — which means that he had given up on her. Because she was trouble.

But now those lips are back again — those incredible lips he's crazy for — those lips he's been denying for the last couple of days — which belong to a fantastic woman he would be a fool to lose!

Suddenly, all the ratfish have lips. And it doesn't matter about the porn. That had only been a test — to see what he could take, to see if he would blow up — but he didn't, he had risen above the situation. And it wasn't too late. What other people thought didn't matter! Her history was irrelevant. He didn't care how much money she had, if she was a movie star, or if she had an asshole or not — Who cares?!

"Hah!" Yann laughs, stretching his back, and looking at the idiot fish in the hold. He laughs again. He laughs at himself, the fish, the crew . . . their seriousness. It just ain't worth it! They can have their shame, but he's not about to play their game. Getting on their bad side was the best move he ever made. It had freed him.

Yann begins to devise his plan. He'll go and see April. He'll apologize to her and be up front with her. He'll see how she's doing, and if she's doing as crummy as he is, then maybe they'll say sayonara together!

Yann had saved up over eight thousand dollars, and soon he'd have a couple thousand more. They could go anywhere, they could do anything. Maybe she would like his crabbing idea, and they could get a truck and drive around in the redwoods together. But then there was her Hawaii idea! He could go for barracuda —

"Hey Fuckhead!" the captain yells down. "Wipe that stupid-ass grin off your face and get up here! We're docking!"

Yann climbs up and into the gray shitty air. Over on the dock he can see the women waiting for them. The ratfish is surrounded by kids with sticks and Nadine is in the crowd, Mother Kralik also. But April is nowhere to be seen.

The captain blows the foghorn twice and pulls up to the pilings. Their boat is the first of six to arrive, the others following close behind.

"Ratfish!" the captain announces to the crowd, as is customary on St. Ratfish Day. "We got ratfish! Not catfish! Not batfish! But ratfish! Come and get yer ratfish on St. Ratfish Day!"

The kids cheer and immediately start hitting the ratfish with their sticks. Garbage flies through the air. The crowd applauds. But still, their cheers are flatter than in years before.

Around the turn of the century, the islanders had done the same thing. The ratfish back then, however, had been bigger and more plentiful, and had been used for oil, which was burned in lamps. It stank. Ratfish had also been used to fertilize crops, which stunk up the fields. Now, however, ratfish had gone to the dogs.

"Ratfish stink! Ratfish stink!" the children howl and go to town on the ratfish. Inside the padded costume, some drunk is taking a thrashing.

Yann grabs his bag and steps off the boat. Since he is taller than most of the people on the island, he can see above their heads. But still, no April.

Yann doesn't blame her though. It was a pretty gruesome scene she'd seen the other day. Maybe she spotted him in the bar and figured he was part of it.

But then he sees her, beyond St. Ratfish, standing on her toes, straining to look above the crowd. And he knows that things are okay, because her eyes are wide and bright and she tosses him a kiss.

Yann makes as if to catch it, then heads her way.

"Come *on!*" Nadine says, and grabs Yann by the arm. She starts to pull him away.

"No," Yann objects.

He looks into her eyes; they're out of control: crimson tendrils circled by black shadows, buggy and bulgy, bouncing in her sockets. And then he sees the claw marks on her face, as if she'd been mauled by a grizzly bear. Nadine is not looking good.

"Look," she tells him, with a harshness rising in her voice, "if you don't wanna talk in private then we'll talk right here about how you *knocked me up and haven't done shit!*"

A few heads turn their way.

"Okay," he agrees, so she doesn't make a big public scene. He follows her into the Dirty Dawgfish. Hans is passed out on the bar. The place is dark and empty.

"Sit down," she tells him, and points to a table in the corner. He sits down.

Nadine puts her hands on her hips and glares at him. "Well," she says, "where is it?"

"Where's what?"

"The ring, dumbshit."

"What ring?"

"You know damn well what ring," she tells him. "You proposed to me, didn't you?!"

"Well . . . kind of."

"What the fuck do you mean kind of?! You want our child to grow up without a fucking father?!"

Yes, Yann thinks, but he doesn't say a thing.

"Answer me, dammit!" Nadine says, raising her voice.

"No," Yann says. He looks over at Hans, snoring away, shitfaced till Tuesday.

"Well, did you propose to me or not?"

"I told you what you wanted to hear."

"Oh, so you were lying?!"

"No," Yann lies. It's been days since he has showered. He's starting to sweat like his father.

"Look," she tells him, "I got some bastard growing inside me, what the fuck do you got?!"

She pulls up her shirt, revealing her belly. It doesn't look any fatter to Yann — but the flesh, that soft belly flesh, it does something to him — even though it terrifies him. What he's got is a boner.

Suddenly the tension between them changes. Nadine knows she can't scare Yann into standing by his word, so she decides to use her most powerful weapon instead — since she senses that he's sensing it.

"You know what else I got?" she asks him.

"What?" he asks.

Nadine lowers her hand beneath her navel and grabs the

waistband of her skirt. She lowers it until the edge of her pubic patch is peeking out. Yann stares at it.

Inserting her hand into her skirt, Nadine feels her way to her slickening lips, like two slaps of liver changing texture. She closes her eyes and imagines her employer's ass: those two glorious moons of meat, the way they quiver when she comes . . .

Nadine starts to secrete. Simultaneously, a drop of presemen squeezes from Yann's dick. The air smells like the musk of his pits.

Then, before Yann can even protest, Nadine is under the table unzipping his fly. His cock pops out, solid and erect. Nadine immediately starts kissing it. Yann does not object.

"You've fucked her, haven't you?" Nadine asks.

"Who?" Yann asks back.

She nibbles his dick, biting it a bit — but not too hard. This frightens Yann, but excites him as well. He knows she won't bite it off because she is a nympho and she wants it.

Nadine laps away like a dog on shit. Yann leans back in his chair and looks at a wad of gum on the ceiling.

"You want to do her in the ass, don't you?" Nadine asks, pausing for a second. "You want to grease up your dick and shove it in her bunghole . . ."

Yann doesn't speak, just leans back, turning her foul mouth off. Whatever she's saying has nothing to do with him — she's just talking dirty again. If he listens to her, he'll lose his erection.

"You want to pork her there, don't you?" Nadine asks, pausing again, then engulfing the whole thing and starting to bob her head up and down. Yann doesn't answer. She

stops again. "Yeah, you want to hose her from behind . . .
Yeah, you want to have your face in there, in her crack . . .
yeah, that's what you want . . ."

Nadine starts to finger herself. When she says these
things to him, all he hears is gibberish ending in the curve
of a question. He is concentrating on coming in her mouth.

Nadine frigs away, increasing the speed in the bob of her
head. Her hormones are going berserk, flashing visions in
her head. She is seeing what she wants to see.

"Yeah, and then you'd lick her all up and down her
crack," Nadine continues, "those soft little hairs . . . she'd
be all sweaty in there . . . yeah, you'd suck up as much as
you could . . . yeah . . . yeah . . ."

"Yeah," Yann says, agreeing with the blow job. He's getting ready to squirt.

Nadine goes back to slurping away. How she manages to
take it all in, he doesn't know. Her mouth is a hot wet hole.
She lifts her head again, still playing with herself.

"And then I take my tongue and jam it in her asshole,"
Nadine says. "I jam it way in there until it touches a turd,
that's how far I jam it in there . . . right?"

"Yeah," Yann says, just to keep her sucking him,
"yeah . . ."

He forces her head back down. He starts to guide it up
and down. He lifts his ass, thrusting and thrusting into her
face. He fucks her face.

Nadine, meanwhile, has reached the apex of her frigging
frenzy. She starts to convulse. She's ripping April's anus
open . . . her tongue is a ramrod . . . April loves it! And so
does Nadine. A torpid fluid courses through her flesh and

she ejaculates — which is something she has never done before, and will never do again.

Yann has no idea what is going on beneath the table. All he knows is that everything's at an all-time max and his jizz is starting to race for —

Nadine pulls back and looks up at Yann. His body is clenched, his teeth are clenched, his eyes are clenched, his face is clenched, but most of all, his balls are clenched. All she has to do is give him a squeeze and he'll erupt like a geyser all over her face.

A cruel smile alights in her mind. Fuck him! Standing up, she smacks her head on the table — having forgotten it was there. It tips over backwards and crashes to the floor, startling Yann and making her reel. White flashes go off in her head. He looks up at her and she looks down at him. She is standing above him, holding her head, and he is sitting below her, holding his pecker.

"Haw haw haw!" she laughs at him, the stripes in her face flushing red with blood. It's that laughter again. *"Haw haw haw haw!"*

Yann's dick immediately goes limp. He watches Nadine turn and walk away, tipping her head and laughing at the sky. *"Haw haw haw haw haw haw haw!"* The door slams behind her.

Yann looks down at his dick full of cum that didn't come. He gives it a few jerks, but it's no use.

"Hey," Hans's voice suddenly says, "when you get through fucking all the tables, be sure to put them right-side up."

Yann stuffs himself back in his pants as the bartender

drops his head to the bar. Immediately, he starts snoring again.

Yann looks around at the emptiness, too ashamed to leave it. What the heck is wrong with him? What the heck is wrong with Nadine? Why'd he let her do that to him? Why'd he even want her to?

Dropping his head into his hands, Yann tries not to blubber like a little puss. But it's useless. He's a fuckup and he knows it. He is one of them.

23

IT'S ANOTHER SUCKY DAY on the island as April scans the beach from her bedroom window, looking through binoculars. There's garbage washed up all over the sand, and dead fish everywhere. She hasn't seen Yann for days, and all she's been doing is sitting around — which is what she does every day.

As for Nadine, she's been acting strange lately, and she didn't really prove to be a very good drinking companion. As for Father O'Flugence, she still doesn't trust the guy. When she went to visit him the other day, she found her flare gun in his closet, beneath a bunch of magazines of gawky adolescent boys. So she stashed the flare gun in her purse without even telling him. Why should she? It was hers, had been in her purse when the boat went down. He'd given her everything back except that and a couple hundred bucks. The crooked old pervert!

She says to herself, what the hell am I doing with these people? Has this town gone completely wacko? Never again will she go to that bar! There's nothing to do and no one to hang out with! And the weather, it sucks!

Then she spots the cove known as Secret Cove, nestled between two rocks a mile past the spit. There's something about that spot: it's sandy and protected, and there isn't any garbage there. It would be a nice place to go for a swim. But not alone, not on this creepy island! There's no telling what some lunatic might do.

April scans past the cove and spots Yann's boat chugging out to sea. She can see him standing on the bow. He's heading out for the Big Run, as they call it.

But why didn't he come to see her yesterday? After that ratfish parade, she'd sat at home like a nervous schoolgirl waiting for him, scribbling hearts and writing their initials inside. And he never showed up.

April hears a knock at the door and puts down the binoculars. For a second she's ecstatic, thinking that maybe Yann stayed behind — but no, she'd seen him out there.

Oh, she remembers, it's just Nadine.

Wrapping her bathrobe tighter around her, April descends and opens the door. Nadine is standing there with a laundry basket. She looks like a mess.

"What happened to your face?" April gasps.

"I ain't been getting much sleep." Nadine glares back, almost accusatory.

"Scabs on your face from lack of sleep?"

"Oh, those," Nadine says. "I gouged those in my face."

"Why?" April asks, staring aghast at her.

"Just cuz," Nadine replies, still glaring at April. There's an awkward moment of silence.

"Well," April eventually says, trying to dismiss Nadine's appearance, "come on in."

April steps back and Nadine enters, plopping the laundry basket on the floor.

"Hmmmm," April utters and kneels down to look in the basket. Her bathrobe opens slightly, revealing some boobage to Nadine — whose mood suddenly changes. Now she doesn't feel resentment anymore, now she feels a longing for what she can't have.

"But these are all wrinkly, Nadine," April says, looking up. "Do you have an iron at your house?"

"Yes," Nadine answers, her arms hanging by her sides. She is starting to cry.

"Oh, Nadine," April says, her voice bending with concern, "what's wrong?"

April stands up and makes a motion to hug Nadine, but Nadine, suddenly, swats her hands away. There's a look on her face like an animal has right before it gnaws off a paw because it's caught in a trap.

Again, they stand there for a prolonged time. April breaks the silence. "Well then," she suggests, "why don't you take this laundry home and iron it, and bring it back when you're done?"

"Okay." Nadine shrugs and picks the basket up. She turns and heads out the door, neither of them saying a word. April closes the door behind her.

"God help me," she says, leaning against the wall. She notices some cobwebs on the ceiling. Later Nadine can get those with a broom.

Nadine heads down the hill, a low rumbling rising from her throat. That bitch! That rich-bitch porn-slut movie cunt! With those fat honking tits! Yeah . . . those fantastic beautiful tits . . .

"Rrrrrrr," Nadine growls, and feels herself getting wet. Or maybe she's finally getting her period, which is long overdue and adding to her conviction that she's preggy. The truth of the matter is that she's had PMS for over a week, and her infection is getting worse.

Nadine swipes a finger under her skirt, runs it across her crotch, and brings it up, smelling it. Nope, it's pussy juice. Dammit, she's horny! Horny to fuck! But Yann's away, and April doesn't give a shit! *Fuck fuck fuck fuck!* Even if it rips her pussy wide open, even if it worsens her infection! FUCK FUCK FUCK FUCK FUCK!

Nadine reaches her trailer and swings the door open. Her mother is there, sitting in a chair, staring at the wall.

"Shut up," Nadine says, but of course she receives no answer.

Lately, Nadine has been slacking off taking her mother to work. *Fuck 'em* is her attitude. If they really want her mom to work, then let them come and get her! She's sick of taking care of the slut-ass bitch!

Nadine sets the basket on the table and sets up the ironing board. She plugs in the iron and waits for it to get hot.

"I could press this into your face," she tells her mother, "and burn your ugly mug right off."

Her mother just sits there, glaring back at her. Nadine

can smell her mother's fear. She could kill the bitch in a flinch but spits on the iron instead. It sizzles. She reaches into the basket and takes out a pair of panties.

Wham! The door bursts open and Mother Kralik comes blasting in. She's wearing a smock splattered with blood.

"Underwear!" Mother Kralik squeals with delight, and snatches the panties from Nadine. Widow Flanahan and Widow O'Reilly follow Mother Kralik in, both of them dressed in sanguine smocks as well.

"Give it back," Nadine says. "What do you want?"

"We just came by," Mother Kralik tells her, "to see why your mother isn't at work."

"If you want her there," Nadine says, "then take her there. Now give it back."

"Such nice nice panties," Mother Kralik says, holding them up for all to see. "Such nice . . . silky . . . delicate panties . . . with such nice . . . pretty . . . delicate lace, so girlish and so frilly . . ."

Nadine's neck twitches twice. She grabs the underwear back.

"Lingerie!" she tells Mother Kralik. "It's lingerie, okay? It ain't underwear!"

"Ooooo!" Mother Kralik responds, feigning respect. "*Lingerie!* Excuuuse me! But, Nadine, since when did you start wearing such fancy-shmancy *lingerie?*"

Nadine doesn't answer. She goes to work ironing it, pressing down on it so hard that the legs of the ironing board begin to bend.

"Since you started seeing what Little Miss Money-Muff struts around the house in?" Mother Kralik asks, the hags behind her chuckling.

"She's paying me to iron 'em," Nadine snaps, "so get off my back!"

"Ooooo!" Mother Kralik says, in a patronizing voice. "I didn't know. I had no idea. I guess I should get with the times, shouldn't I? It's just that we've never had a *serrrvant* on the island before. Leastwise not a white one!"

The crones cackle. Even Nadine's mother adds a snort of laughter.

Nadine's neck twitches again. She burns a stare across the underwear and into Mother Kralik's face. The stare is meant to murder her.

Thwack! Mother Kralik slaps Nadine a good one in the face and grabs the underwear back. Nadine sets the iron down and rubs her face.

"Don't you ever look at me like that again, you little kiss-ass bitch!" Mother Kralik howls. "Next time you do . . . I'll wipe your ass right off of this planet! I'll destroy you with a single thought! Got it?!"

Nadine lowers her head and nods. The more she humors the old bag, the sooner she'll take a hike.

"Behold, sisters!" Mother Kralik says, turning toward the widows and holding April's panties above her head. "The underwear of a whore! Or, to be more precise, the *lingerie* of the Devil's whore! See how it goes right up the crack of her ass?!"

Mother Kralik sniffs the underwear. "Ahhh, so pleasantly perfumed! Ahhh yes, you see . . . the cunt of the Devil's whore, it doesn't stink like the cunt of a slut! It smells like a tulip! Yes indeed, a charming little tulip!"

Mother Kralik changes her hold on the underwear, pinching it between her fingers. She holds it out like a turd and scans the faces in the room.

"Of course," she tells them, "there's only one solution about what to do with the *lingerie* of the Devil's whore! There's only one way to fully remove that false fake tulipy smell, you know! You gotta burn it out!"

Mother Kralik picks up the iron and presses it into the underwear. All of them watch as smoke starts to rise and twist. A burnt smell fills the room as Mother Kralik lifts the iron. The panties are scorched beyond repair.

"Rrrrrr . . ." Nadine growls.

"And the same goes for the whore!" Mother Kralik continues. "To free a whore from her tulip-smelling cunt, there's only one way to do it! You gotta burn the whore! Burn the whore!"

Mother Kralik pauses and glares at Nadine.

"Unless," she adds, "you prefer to give up your soul for the oh-so-flowery waft of tulips in bloom."

The old women cackle as they crowd around to see the ruined underwear.

"Hmmm," Mother Kralik adds, dramatically pretending to sniff the air, "that's funny. Something smells like dead fish in here!" She turns to Nadine. "Do you got a nasty crotch infection, honey, or is your cunt just becoming rotten like ours?"

"Fuck you!" Nadine bursts out, surprised to hear herself reply with the most juvenile of all retorts. "Leave me alone!"

"Okay then," Mother Kralik calmly responds and takes Widow Murphy's hand. "All you had to do was ask . . ."

The women step out of the trailer, leaving Nadine twitching in the kitchen.

"Rrrrrrr!" She shudders and tries to force herself to laugh — but her salvation doesn't matter anymore.

24

APRIL IS IN HER KITCHEN slicing melons when suddenly the sun comes out. The daylight shocks her — it seems completely artificial. She puts down her knife and stares up at the sky. A moment ago it was gray and cruddy, threatening to rain. But now it's as sunny as Southern Californy.

Then something else happens that is out of the ordinary. She hears a truck rumbling up the street. Sometimes they rumble down by the docks, but she's never heard one in front of her house. So she goes to the door to check it out.

There's a rickety old truck pulling up across the street. Some men are getting out, and then a dashing gentleman, followed by an astonishing blonde about the same age as Nadine. Immediately, the men start unloading the truck: sofas, chairs, boxes, trunks . . .

April is so excited she almost pees. Neighbors! Thank God! She rushes back to the kitchen, slices the melon in a jiffy, arranges the pieces on a plate, runs out the door, then crosses her lawn.

As April approaches, she slows to a walk and watches the gentleman direct the workmen, now unloading canvases. He's pointing his stogie at places along the fence where he wants them to be. All of them are nudes of men, and not very good.

"Yooo–hooo!" April calls to them. The two newcomers turn and look her way.

"Hi," April says. "I live across the street, and I see you're moving in. Can I offer you some fresh fruit?"

The girl is instantly starstruck. "Oh my God!" she cries in an Aussie accent. "It's April Berger! I can't believe it! Is that who you are?"

"Well, kind of," April answers and holds the platter out to them. "I came here to escape the madness of the media. I was starting to feel like Lady Di, if you know what I mean."

The gentleman remains stoic. "No, thank you," he answers, apparently out of touch with pop culture. He goes back to directing the workers. They're wrestling a piano into the house.

"Careful now, careful now," he calls to them and heads in their direction to get in their way and make them nervous by hanging over their shoulders.

"Don't mind Daddy," the girl tells April, trying not to show her awe. "He's socially uncoordinated. He's a painter."

"Lovely," April replies. "And what about you?"

"Oh, I'm just a silly little teenager whose personality hasn't been fully formed yet. Every year Daddy comes here to paint the sea, but this year I begged him to take me."

"Oh, I just love your accent," April tells her. "What's your name?"

"Suzanne," she answers, blushing.

"Well," April says, "have some honeydew, Honeydew."

They both giggle, and Suzanne accepts. A montage ensues: Knowingly, their eyes shyly brush each other's. Lashes flash. Enticingly, April raises a piece of melon to her mouth, while Suzanne, delicately, touches her lips to her own. April sees Suzanne seeing her seeing her, and Suzanne sees April seeing the same. Suzanne licks her cube of fruit, then closes her lips around it. April does exactly the same — and it disappears in a kiss. They chew. Cheekbones rise. No language is exchanged.

It is fitting, then, that a few hours later April and Suzanne are down in Secret Cove, rubbing lotion on each other and letting the sun lick their skin. They are topless, of course, as nubile nymphs tend to be in the fantasies of lusty men who love the lines of luscious maids.

And it is fitting, also, that Nadine, having returned with a basket of ironed lingerie, should wonder where her mistress is — so, raising her binoculars, scans the beach.

"Rrrrrr!" she growls, when her vision alights upon the cove. There are four perfect breasts in the air, two of which she has never seen before. They're not as big as April's, but they're bountiful and firm. No doubt, Nadine deduces, they belong to the daughter of that faggot across the street.

"That dyke!" she sneers and zooms in as close as she can. The two half-naked bodies are glistening with oil. And then she sees them sitting up and popping the cork on a bottle of champagne. They are laughing away and having a good old time.

"Rrrrrr!" Nadine growls again. April's teeth are all over the place. She's happy as a clam — down there with that tramp! With her nice ripe tits and her bright yellow hair — things Nadine doesn't have — things, which, if she had, it would be her down there instead of that tramp!

"Rrrrrrr!" Nadine sees them talking to each other, all bright-eyed and bushy-tailed, flapping their wrists and gesturing away, laughing so hard they hold their sides — while she is expected to dust the damn place!

Then she sees them go for the grapes. At first they play a little game, tossing them into each other's mouths. Both of them are poor shots, though — never hitting their targets but always hitting each other's breasts. And every time a tit is hit, they laugh like vixens, they laugh like whores! And then they begin to feed each other.

"Fucking tarts!" Nadine whispers, touching herself. They're rolling the grapes around in their mouths, showing each other how they suck cock! Nadine knows she can suck cock better than them. If they all had a Yann in front of them, she'd be the first to make him come.

"Oh *great!*" Nadine spits and steadies her hand. The smaller slut is lying back against April now, resting her head between those double-D tits and opening her mouth like a blow-job whore. April starts to feed the little trollop! What?! Oh my fucking God! —

Nadine raises the binoculars with the intent to smash them against the floor, but decides not to. She goes back to watching what she can't believe she is seeing — simultaneously reaching into the drawer. She knows where April hides it, so she immediately takes it out and starts it up. It hums. Nadine doesn't wait an instant. She plunges it into her swollen cunt.

"Rrrrrr!" she growls, clenching the binoculars even tighter, feeling the vibrations in her core. "You fucking lesbo bitch!"

Down on the beach, it looks like the gals are getting frisky, but really all it is is play. It's play for April, stroking Suzanne's hair, feeding her grapes, one by one. It's play as they emit intermittent utterings of utter satiation, half-naked on the sand in the rays of the day. It's play as April makes a perfect grape dance on Suzanne's perfect breast — as a perfect nipple rises, taking form, and April's hardens just as well. It's play.

April has no intention of seducing Suzanne, and Suzanne, the youngest of five sisters who grew up playing naked with each other on the beaches of Perth, sees this as a sisterly thing. If either of them is getting excited, it's because they're giddy from being together, and the champagne. They are only pretending, even though the warmth cannot be denied — the warmth of flesh against flesh.

"Come on," Suzanne says, and jumps up, "let's swim!"

She sheds her shorts and runs into the waves, leaping in with hardly a splash. April follows, tossing her bottoms onto the sand. They bounce around in the surf, ducking under waves, laughing their asses off.

A little fish swims by, and Suzanne screams. She isn't really frightened by it — but it's an excuse to continue their flirtation. She leaps toward April, acting like a girly girl.

"A fish! A fish!" Suzanne shouts, affecting fear. She

wraps her naked self around her new friend's nudity —
providing the occasion for supposed throes coupled with
erotic moans — as April plays along, writhing and groping
back, giggling at their little game — which they embellish
with urgent squirms in the brine.

Then a wave comes curling toward them, so they duck
beneath it. And when they come up, April's lips are pressed
to a breast of Suzanne's. She blows on it, making a fart
noise. Both of them laugh like crazy, and April can't help
it — she pees in the sea.

Up in April's window, however, the laughter is of a different nature. It's that mad laughter of Nadine. She is stabbing the vibrator — into her! and into her! and into her! —
like a dagger, aggravating her infection.

Then, when she comes, she lets loose a bloodcurdling
cry and jerks all around like an adulteress getting stoned in
the town square of some Arab village.

"Aiiiiiiiii-Yiiiiiii-Yiiiiiiiii!" Nadine screams, and pulls
the vibrator out. THERE is pinkness on its skin, but it
isn't menstrual blood. It is blood from severe agitation.

HATE HATE HATE!

Nadine doesn't even wipe it off but sticks it back in the
drawer. She looks through the binoculars again. Out in the
waves, they are still dancing around like little bimbos, no
doubt fingering each other.

HATE HATE HATE HATE HATE!

Nadine can't watch anymore — she storms across the
room and stops in front of April's dressing table. Peering
into the mirror, she despises what she sees.

"What the hell are you looking at, you ugly bitch?!" she challenges it, but of course it only mimics her. Next to Nadine's sneering reflection, there's a photo of April taped to the glass, tossing back her silky hair, showing off her Cover Girl skin.

"Rrrrrr!" Nadine growls, attempting to copy the pose, but she can't get the posture right. She stares at the picture. April has wide gorgeous eyes. Nadine has little pisshole eyes. April is tall and statuesque. Nadine is short and squat like a trash can.

"Rrrrrr!" Nadine grabs her face and tries to stretch it out. It doesn't work. She tries to hold her eyes wide open, but when she lets them go they return to their original shape. She hitches up her boobs, but they don't get any bigger.

"Rrrrr! Rrrrrr! Rrrrr," Nadine snarls and sees her neck begin to twitch. It's starting up again goddammit!

She starts tearing through April's makeup, smearing eyeliner all over her face, and then some rouge. It doesn't work — she looks like the sloppiest whore in town.

Grabbing a jar of cold cream, she lifts it high — but again catches herself. She looks at it, defenseless in her hand. It can't do shit, it can't even object! She squeezes it, it breaks. Cold cream, mixed with blood, oozes from between her fingers.

"Haw haw haw haw haw!" She laughs at the ceiling — then wipes her hand on the mirror as if she were smearing shit on it. Nadine laughs again. She laughs and laughs and laughs and laughs. She laughs herself silly. She laughs like the Devil.

25

TWENTY-THREE MILES OUT, Yann and the others are laying their nets across the projected run of the salmon. This is the Big Run, when the fishermen haul in tons of illegal coho and king, which, legally, only the Native Alaskans have the right to fish for. But who's going to do anything about it? The U.S. Coast Guard, the Japanese? NATO? Nope . . . nobody! And so the fishermen string out their nets, as they've been doing since the 1800s.

None of the sailors except the captain will talk to Yann. If One Eye warms up, then there's a chance that the men will take him back — but by that time Yann plans on being long gone. After this run, he's heading straight to April.

April! He can see her clear as day: her lips, those lips — more powerful than alcohol! He truly believes that he will die if he never gets to kiss those lips. He must kiss those lips to live!

But it's not just those lips that have become those lips, it's also what's attached to them: the woman he is obsessed with, the woman he is in love with. And he plans on telling

her so. He'll march right up to her and be honest with her.
And she'll either accept his love or reject it. And that will
be his destiny.

"Hey, Fuckferbrains!" The captain scowls. "I thought
you were on watch!"

"I am," Yann says, turning toward him.

"Then what the fuck's that?!"

Yann looks out and sees a dark cloud. It extends from
one end of the horizon to the other.

"It must be that heavy weather coming back," he says.
"Looks like the sun only lasted a couple hours."

"Well if it isn't," the captain barks, "it's your ass!"

Little do the fishermen know, El Niño has come early
this year. Already, it has wiped out a village in El Salvador,
leaving over three thousand people either dead or missing,
and has gone out to the Pacific, where it bumped into an er-
rant typhoon, then bounced off and took a right. And as it
roars north toward the Bering Strait — a tempest of gale-
force winds, tidal waves, and Russian destruction in its
wake — snow falls before it and behind it. It is heading for
the North Pole, where it will eventually skate across the ice
and unfurl in the vast white soundlessness, as if it never
was.

Yann watches the boats spreading out. There are six of
them, with five-mile-long nets connecting them. The
salmon have no chance. Already he can see them coming,
leaping and splashing toward their boats, just like every
year before. These, however, are the first of thousands.
More will follow, racing for the rivers of their birth.

But, suddenly, they change their course. Yann sees it

happen. They turn around and go back. This has never happened before.

"Hey!" Yann yells. "Something's wrong!"

None of the men answers him, but they shoot him dirty looks. He's lucky he's not down in the bilge, so he better shut up and open his mouth only if something's up. His job is to keep watch for other boats, or dangerous weather — none of the boats being equipped with radar.

So Yann goes back to watching the storm. No doubt it will be just as much a drag as it has been for the last couple days, menacing and miserable, but harmless.

Yann looks through the telescope and watches the horizon. As the black line begins slinking closer, he feels a tightening in his gut. He doesn't know why, but he figures it's because this storm resembles the storm that took Bubba out. But that storm won't be back for another year.

The approaching cruddiness, however, is something that none of the fishermen can fathom. Above it, there are squiggly lines bending the air. And the temperature is dropping. It is different, something they have never seen before. Yann calls the captain over.

"Take a look through the scope," Yann tells him. "It looks kinda funny."

"Look," the captain says, "don't bother me with that fucking shit! You think I don't know fucking rain clouds when I fucking see 'em?! You think I just fell off the fucking turnip fucking truck?! Stop fucking bugging me, fuckface!"

Yann shrugs and watches the skyline. The thing is getting bigger, blacker, faster. There's a white mist in front of it, visible through the telescope but not to the naked eye. Yann recognizes what it is, though. It's snow.

Now Yann's sure they're about to get smeared. He stands up and clangs the bell, sounding the alarm.

"What?!" The captain comes around the cabin yelling. "What the fuck, fucking shitfuck?!"

"That's no ordinary storm!" Yann says. "We gotta turn the radio on!"

The captain rolls his eyeballs. "We ain't got no fucking radios that fucking work, you fucking fuck! You know that!"

"Well take a look," Yann says, trying to hand him the telescope again. "I'm telling you. We're gonna get it!"

"If it gets fucked up, then we'll fucking turn fucking back," the captain tells him with a bit of compassion in his voice. "But you know as well as me . . . you don't fucking go out and fucking run your fucking nets, then close up shop till you start getting fucking fucked with!"

The captain turns around and goes back to the cabin to snort some more bathtub crank. It's the Bubba Murphy school of fishing again. Yann knows there's nothing he can do, so he straps on his life jacket just to make a point.

"Haw haw!" One Eye yucks. "Look at fucking Fuck-nuts!"

All the fishermen laugh at Yann.

They aren't laughing half an hour later, though, when the flurry comes flying at them — horizontally. Then, suddenly, all of them are wearing life vests.

The captain comes out of the cabin, wiping at his nose,

flashing his eyes all over the place. The whole crew is watching the skyline. It's a few miles away and rolling toward them, looking like a flash flood of mud, as far as the eye can see.

"Fucking Jesus!" the captain swears. "What sort of a front is that!"

The temperature drops like a rock, from seventy-three to thirty-three degrees in less than a minute.

"Haul in the fucking nets!" the captain orders. The men start hauling ass. There are battered seagulls in the nets. The water gets green and slushy.

Pretty soon, the snow is sticking to the boat and all the equipment. It gets so thick they can hardly see six feet in front of them. They are in a blizzard at sea.

But then the snow is replaced by rain, equally horizontal. Now the men can see, but what they see is not encouraging. The other boats are hauling up as well, because the monster is upon them: ten times taller than King Kong, and blacker than his asshole.

"Jesus fuck!" the captain yells. "Where the fuck did this come from?! Yann! What the fuck were you doing?!"

Yann doesn't answer him. It is churning above them, darker than the smoke of a thousand flaming freighters, roiling like a chemical blaze, holding in its muffled combustion — an electrical nightmare so devoid of light that the blasts inside can be heard roaring like jet engines but cannot be seen — as the whole charged mass searches for something to attach itself to: anything sticking up from the vast ocean below.

Bllammm! Lightning leaps out and strikes the first boat.

It immediately starts burning. The second boat sets off for the first, as Yann and One Eye stand side by side. They are on the sixth boat, all of them connected by a line of nets.

Yann picks up the telescope as the rain pounds his face. The second boat is having trouble getting to the first boat because its connection to the third is preventing it from moving forward. The second boat is kicking up black smoke, tugging on the nets dogging its progress, and the first boat is going down.

"Let me see that!" the captain growls, and grabs the telescope from Yann. He sees the men on the first boat piling into the lifeboat and then men on the second boat slashing at the net lines as the sky continues to unleash its fire, striking again and again at the red-hot mast, drilling itself into the ship.

A flare is fired from the lifeboat, but nobody hears it because of the thunder. The flaming ship is half-sunk, and everyone knows that, when it's gone, the sky will look for another node to dump its fury into.

"Cut the ropes!" the captain yells. "Fire up the engine!"

"All the ropes?" One Eye asks.

"All the motherfucking ropes!" the captain orders.

Yann runs to the starboard side and gets out his knife. He starts in slashing at the ropes, which are over an inch thick. It's a tedious process. The first boat has almost gone down and is starting to pull the second one under. Yann hacks away like a madman while One Eye just stands there playing pocket pool.

Then there is darkness and wind. The sun is gone and the sea is rougher. A sudden roller comes up from nowhere and washes across the deck. Yann holds on as the boat teeters. It's going over, just like before.

"Noooooooooo!" One Eye screams, and grabs on to Yann. He clings to him as the boat rights itself and leans the other way. Yann uses these few seconds to shove One Eye off and sever the rope he's working on. Then he moves on to the next one.

Blammm! Lightning hits the boat closest to theirs. Yann sees it in the flash lasting a second, and then it's gone in the darkness. The captain comes out of the hold with a chain saw.

"What the hell are you doing?!" One Eye yells.

"I'm chopping down the mast!" the captain yells back.

Like all the jimmy-rigged fishing ships of the island, theirs is a sailboat that's been patched and repatched, and is driven by an inboard motor. It is unethical, of course, for a captain to take down his own mast, thus upping the odds that the others will get hit, but it's also an act of survival. Another wave hits the boat.

"GodFuckingFuckFuckingDammit!" the captain yells, pulling the rip cord. "Get the stern to the waves!"

He is shouting at everyone, but no one in particular. Yann figures he better get in the cabin and drive the boat — considering that the captain has taken on another job.

"Here!" Yann says, handing One Eye his knife. One Eye takes it without a response. Yann doesn't know if this is pride or fear or stupidity — but none of that matters now. One Eye knows what he's supposed to do, and so does Yann. When the keel settles, he dives into the cabin, grabs the wheel, and wrestles it to the right — just as a wave comes washing over the transom, pushing the boat ahead in its crest.

"Start the pumps!" the captain shouts.

Yann looks out and over his shoulder. The sea is an immense toilet, starting to swirl. Soon it will flush them into the abyss.

"Gnnnnnnnnnnnnnnnnnnnnnnnnnnnnnnyyyyrrrr!"

Yann hears the captain laying into the mast, which is aluminum with steel underneath. Whether or not the chain saw can cut through it, Yann has no idea. He sees a blaze of sparks and feels the teeth tearing away. The vibrations go right through the floorboard and into his nuts. Into everybody's nuts.

"Motherfucking shitfucking *fuck!*" the captain swears, and keeps on grinding away. Yann opens up the throttle full bore, but the nets are still tight, and One Eye is doing a crummy job at cutting the lines.

"Come on!" Yann yells at One Eye and jumps out of the cabin. "You drive!"

One Eye glares at Yann, refusing to move. Sparks rain down in the darkness as they feel the lift of another wave below them. One Eye won't budge.

Yann moves fast, throwing One Eye into the cabin and grabbing back his knife. All One Eye knows is that the boat is wavering, so he grabs the wheel and points the bow the direction of the tell-tales — which he can see because of the sparks. The prop is out of the water and revving to the red line.

Krrrr-powww! Lightning hits the ship, and everyone feels the charge. One Eye's heart almost stops, but doesn't.

The captain's, however, is another story. The current goes right down the mast, into the chain saw, and into his aorta. He drops dead on the spot, the chain saw falls out of his hands, and the mast bends and collapses, snapping stays and cables all over the boat.

There are three other members of the crew, but where they are Yann doesn't know. The chain saw is spinning on the deck. He dives for it and grabs it with the agility of an athlete who sees something happen the split second it occurs and acts just as fast. In less than a second it's in his hands and he is mowing through the ropes holding back the boat. He feels the engine grip the ocean.

Lester comes up from the hold and flicks the deck lights on, just as Yann hits the kill button, turning off the chain saw.

"We got the pumps running," he tells Yann, as if Yann is the captain. "Charlie and Fred are running 'em! We gotta lotta water down there!"

Yann looks up at the captain, now a pile of squashed meat. The mast is on top of him, and he is smoking from his fingertips. Yann reaches up and feels his wrist. No pulse. The boat rises once again. They are beneath the crest of a colossal wave, which is rising and rising and rising above them, while bearing down on them at the same time.

"Help! Help!" One Eye cries, letting go of the wheel, then grabbing it again. He's freaking out.

"Captain's dead," Yann yells at Lester. "Go down and get Charlie, tell him to come up here and drive the boat!"

Lester does what he is told. Yann has appointed himself captain, to no one's objection. At least he can think, and what he thinks is that One Eye is doing a lame-ass job at steering the boat.

Charlie comes up and flicks on the running lights. He's a forty-five-year-old alcoholic who had gone down to Big Sur as a teenager, lived the life of a surfer dude, and competed in some national competitions. He'd done all right for a while, but then he started dealing coke. He got busted, jumped bail, and came back to the island. Yann figures he'd be better than anyone else onboard at riding the wave.

"Get in there and drive this sucker!" Yann orders Charlie, and Charlie obeys. One moment later One Eye is out and clinging to the deck, glaring at Yann for firing him.

Meanwhile, Charlie is putting the boat to the left. Everything begins to tip, and again One Eye reaches out and grabs for Yann. Yann wraps an arm around him and holds on to the rail with the other hand. For a second they hover almost upside-down, waiting to drop into the sea. One Eye stares his hate into Yann, and Yann stares blankly back at him.

"We're going down, you fucking piece of fucking shit, and it's all your fucking fault!" One Eye screams, and loses his grip on Yann. Yann, however, holds on to him as well as the rail.

The next thing they know, they're shooting the tube.

"Yaaa-Hoooo!" Charlie howls, and the boat levels out.

One Eye disengages from Yann and pushes himself away. Yann, however, is watching the mast, which is still attached by a thin strip of metal. The deck is at an angle, and the mast is slipping. Only a few measly ropes are holding it, including one about to snap —

"Duck!" Yann yells in One Eye's face, but One Eye

won't. He just scowls back at Yann, who drops to the deck. *Snap!* The mast swings down, hitting One Eye like a baseball bat, knocking his head completely off.

Yann screams as he watches it sail into the sea, followed by a fountain of blood. One Eye's body loses its grip and slips off the deck. When it vanishes with the mast, its neck is still spewing away, like a killer whale clearing its blowhole.

26

APRIL AND SUZANNE HEAD BACK because it's getting cold. When they reach their homes, they exchange kisses and plan to get together soon. Dark clouds start to roll in.

"Hello, Nadine!" April calls as she walks into her house, but Nadine doesn't answer.

She must be gone, April figures and heads to her answering machine. There are several blinks, indicating messages. She pushes the button. It's her agent, Larry:

"Listen, April . . . they've been coming down hard on me, I had to tell them where you were and how to get ahold of you. It's about Ronson. I told you they'd be wanting to contact you. Who's they? I'll tell you who. The FBI, that's who! I'm sure you'll hear from them shortly if you haven't already. Look, what am I supposed to do over here, just wire you money whenever you want it? What good does that do me? If you're not making any dough, I'm not making dookie! Give me a call soon. See ya, babe."

The dial tone follows. Then three or four hang-ups.

April tries to star-69 the hang-ups but can't. The island doesn't have that technology yet. (Little does she know, these calls were from the FBI, trying to find out if she is in fact on the island, because an agent is on his way to interview her — but not like Geraldo would. A billionaire is missing.)

April bites her lower lip, then heads upstairs to rinse the salt off her skin. She walks into the bathroom, flicks on the light, pulls down her bikini bottoms, and plants her ass on the toilet. She starts to tinkle, then looks between her legs.

"Noooo!!" April screams and jumps up pissing. In the toilet is Poo-poo, but not the human kind. It's her kitten — with a cord around its neck, stiff with rigor mortis.

April falls into the bathtub and lies there with her heart beating erratically. She is petrified. What the hell is wrong with these people? Are they out to get her? Are they in the house right now? And who, in particular, would do such a thing?

"Poo-poo," she whispers and lies there peeing. After a while, though, she gets up, pulls her bottoms up, and tiptoes to her room. She flicks on the light, expecting an ax in the face, but all she sees is a giant, bloody cold cream smear on her mirror, and the words DIE BITCH! written in it.

April reaches into her dresser drawer. She pulls out her flare gun.

Slowly, she goes around the house turning on the lights and holding her gun like they taught her to do in *Copchick*, that box-office bomb in which she played a big-busted chick-dick named Cleavage Heat. Everything, however, looks pretty normal.

After locking all the doors and latching all the windows, she sits down in the kitchen and wonders what to do. She can't call the police, because there are none. And she still doesn't trust that Father O'Flugence, or even Nadine. Yann is the only person on the island she feels she can turn to, but he is out at sea.

The only logical thing to do, April decides, is to go to Suzanne and her father across the street. But what if it was her father who did this? He didn't seem to be very friendly toward women.

Then April remembers the hang-ups on the answering machine. Oh shit! she thinks, I'm being stalked! She knows she has to get the hell out of this place; with or without her grandmother's cross, with or without Elphy or Bun-bun or any of them, with or without saying good-bye to Yann, or Suzanne, but with her life!

She stands up and goes to the liquor cabinet, gets a bottle of whiskey out, and pours herself a shot. It steadies her nerves, so she has another. There's only one thing to do: go to sleep with her flare gun by her side, shoot any intruders, and hope to make it till morning. Then she'll go down to the docks with cash in hand and hire a boat to take her away from this grotesque burlesque, where the bars are primal brothels of spite, where girls claw themselves in the face and the priest is a pervert!

April begins to feel pretty good about her decision. She knows she's tough and admires herself for keeping it together. She takes the flare gun and marches upstairs to her room. She gets dressed without even looking at the mirror, and then, when she's ready, gets some rags and wipes the cold cream off. Now she feels even stronger than before, to be able to operate under such conditions. Other women would've just pissed in their pants, but not her! Besides, she assures herself, this was the work of a coward, not a killer. If somebody really wanted her dead, they would've already done it. Obviously, someone was just trying to scare her . . .

April fishes Poo-poo out of the toilet. She takes the cat outside and buries it as fast as she can, then runs back in and bolts the door behind her.

A few minutes later she hears a knock and feels her bladder quiver. She holds back the urge to pee, grips the flare gun, and looks through the peephole. She sees Suzanne hugging a blanket and a pillow. April opens the door.

"Hi!" Suzanne sings, bouncing into the house. April locks the door behind her and tries not to throw her arms around her and tell her all that has transpired. It might scare the poor little thing — and maybe there's no reason for that.

"I asked Daddy if I could come spend the night at your place, since we had such a great time at the beach today and our house is such a mess," Suzanne tells April. "Do you think that would be okay?"

April thinks about it for a second. She'd love to have the company, and it'd make her feel a whole lot safer to have someone with her. And it's not like she has to tell Suzanne the scurvy details, that'd just make things worse. She could fake it, being an actress and all.

"Why I'd love that," April says, a hardly audible false-ness in her voice. "I'd just love it."

Then Suzanne sees the gun and looks questioningly at April.

"Oh that?" April says. "That's just a flare gun, you know. I use it on the Fourth of July. I was just cleaning it."

"Oh, of course." Suzanne smiles and walks into the room. She knows April is full of shit, having never been a very good actress. But that doesn't matter. All that matters to her is hanging out with April Berger!

April goes and gets some wine, and pretty soon they're listening to Sting and singing along with the Police. April brings down Elphy and Bun-bun, and they make them dance around and converse, saying silly animal things. April begins to feel a lot less on edge. Then they both start to yawn.

"I could sleep down here on the couch," Suzanne says, making her statement sound like a question.

"Oh nonsense," April tells her. "We'll sleep together in my bed."

Suzanne nods excitedly. There's nothing she would rather do than snuggle up with April. So that's what they do, after putting their nightgowns on and brushing their teeth. Right before they shut off the lights, however, Suzanne sees April stash the gun beneath the bed.

Then suddenly they're spooning. April is on the outside.

"April?" Suzanne whispers.

"What is it, Honeydew?" April asks.

"I really really really had a great time today. I'm so glad you're on the island."

"Awww, that's sweet, Sweetie," April tells her. "I'm really really really glad to know you too, and I'm really really really glad you're here."

"Really?

"Yes, really really really really!"

"April?"

"Yes?"

"I really really really think you're cool."

April squeezes Suzanne, and both of them giggle, then drift off. They don't even hear the rain start to fall. They don't even hear the wind begin to scream through the trees. They are beat from sun and fun, visions of sugarplums dancing in their heads.

27

NADINE STORMS THROUGH THE STORM — first
through the snow, then through the rain. She's
hysterical, raging through the blackness and the
hard wet wind, laughing at the unseasonal sky. The sky,
however, is not laughing back. It is flinging things, sometimes almost blowing her over. But Nadine doesn't care.
She has totally lost it.

She doesn't know where she is, who she is, why she's doing what she's doing, or why her neck is twitching like it is.
She doesn't know what time it is, what day it is, or why
she's out on the street, and then on the beach, yelling,
"Die, bitch! *Die, bitch!*" into the wind.

She doesn't even know who she wants to die. All she
knows is that's it time for someone to pay!

A shack appears. It's Mother Kralik's, and candles are
burning inside. She goes to a window and peers into the
warmth. All the hags are sitting there, playing cards and
boozing hard. Even her mother is there. Nadine starts to
remember.

Yann! April! That little slut! It's a conspiracy! Her mother's in on it! Mother Kralik started it! The cat! Oh yes, the cat! That was a good one with the cat! *"Die, bitch!"* That was good too! She knocks on the door.

Mother Kralik opens it, and Nadine steps in with at least half a gallon of rain. The door slams behind her. She is soaking wet.

"Well, well, well," Mother Kralik says, "if it isn't Cinderella! Shouldn't you be home catching up on your sleep, so you can scrub tomorrow?"

Nadine glares at Mother Kralik, and Mother Kralik sees a fucked up kid with a fucked up face, drenched to the bone and crazy-eyed to boot.

Mother Kralik starts in: "Where've you been? Sucking dog dick?!"

"Yeah!" Nadine says. "I was sucking dog dick. You should try it sometime, it's the only dick you'll ever get, you ugly old bat! *Haw haw haw haw!*"

For a second, Mother Kralik's eyes go wide, but then she nods with approval. Everything is like she planned. She knows the girl is weak and easily manipulated, but she didn't think she'd break so soon.

"Sit down," Mother Kralik invites. "Get drunk, get loose! Everybody! Now's the time to get ripped like never before! I'm talking *fucked up!*"

Nadine sits down and starts slamming shots. They all slam shots, and exchange taunts that would make the roughest sailors feel uneasy.

"Fuck me?! Fuck you! You listen to me, Cuntfart!"

"Piece of dogshit! Piece of dogshit!"

"Assfuck! Assfuck! Diarrhea!"

The candlelight flickers. Birds bash against the windows. Branches fall and hit the roof. Rain streams in. The storm howls at the seams of the shack.

"Beershit! Cockshit! Fuckshit!"

"Bloody Pus-covered Miscarriage!"

"Tampon Face!"

"Douche-Bag Breath!"

"Squidshit! Suck my squidshit!"

"Haw haw haw haw haw!"

Hedonism! Rotten teeth! Awful horrid gory laughter! Turgid twisted wrinkled grimaces! The women continue taunting each other.

"Wormshit!"

"Grubshit!"

"Crabshit!"

"Snailshit!"

A dead rat lands on the table. Someone cuts it up. Nadine stands up, falls down. Somebody pukes. A fight starts up. Mother Kralik screeches with glee. Furniture tips over, plaster falls from the ceiling.

Skrrreeeeeeeee! Blaffffffff! Krrrrrrrsssssshhhhhh!

Thunder! Lightning! Crashing smashing bashing sounds! The rain beats against the walls. Salt water washes under the door. Nadine's mother sits there like a tombstone. A flaming punch is brought to the table. The rat's blood is squeezed into it. They drink like pledges at a fraternity kegger.

> Lightning!
> > Thunder!
> > > Fire!
> > > > Laughter!

Nadine finds herself on the floor, once again trying to get up. All the women laugh at her as she laughs back at them. The walls spin, her neck goes hyper, twitching away like never before. Her eyes shoot back in her head.

Slap! Mother Kralik slaps Nadine, trying to bring her back. Nadine comes back, and Mother Kralik makes her drink even more. Nadine spits it up, but chugs as much as she can. She goes into a seizure. The women laugh even harder. What a show!

"You little shitwipe!"

"Hey, fucking fucko!"

"Eat shit and die!"

"Maggotshit!"

Nadine can't take it. She jumps up shuddering and zigs her way to the door. She lunges and lurches and makes it outside, falling down on the sand. The tide has come up five or six feet. The tempest blows in, screaming from the sea. Nadine tries to cling to a tree. Island shrapnel blows all around her. A fish slaps her in the face as her body continues to jerk and quirk volcanically. She bites her tongue, her heart kicks her chest. She falls down on the sand and continues shorting out. She shudders for a bit, gets her breathing under control, then holds her head, trying to keep the madness in.

"Rrrrrrrrrrrrrr! . . . Rrrrrrrrrrrrrrrrr!" Nadine growls, louder and harder and fiercer than before. She knows it's time to laugh, she has to laugh. If she doesn't laugh, she'll kill herself . . . She'll kill someone by God!

But *no!* No more laughing! Her laughing days are over! They're done! She's sick of laughing, sick of denying, sick of pretending! Sick of being sick of being sick! Nadine screams. She screams her fucking lungs out:

"GGGNNNNYYYYYYAAAAAAAARRRRRRKKKKKKK!!!
"FFFFNNNNNYYYYYYYAAAAARRRRRKKKKKKK!!!
"PFFFFFHHHHHHAAAAAARRRRRRKKKKKKK!!!"

And the storm screams back, just as demented. They scream at each other and it builds — bursting and blasting and cracking between them. Water washes all around her. Nature in delirium!

Nadine turns and aims herself at the door. She lurches in drenched again, and so does a wave filled with crabs. They scatter and clatter across the floor, clicking claws across the wood.

The hags shriek like a bunch of buzzards. Widow Flanahan bites Widow O'Reilly. Someone breaks a bottle against the window. They grab things away from each other and spit and snarl and wail like the Dead. They booze like barbarians, drinking past oblivion.

Mother Kralik gets in Nadine's face and starts spouting off about her mother — how she doesn't take care of the bitch. Nadine can't understand the rabid hag, but she knows that this is the face that raped her: With a candle! A cig! A bottle up her cunt!

Mother Kralik increases her harangue. Now she's not doing it for the reason she started, now she's doing it to keep the upper hand. There's something in this little slut that just doesn't give a damn — there's a look on her face — a sneer that goes deeper than nineteen years could ever go. She has been transformed by the storm.

"You never feed her!" Mother Kralik hollers in her face. "You never clean her! She's your motherfucking mother, you stupid cunt!"

Mother Kralik goes on. She knows that screaming at Nadine can only buy her time. When she runs out of breath, Nadine will have the power. The little bitch is more than free, she's in control, because she doesn't have control, because she doesn't give a shit — because she's willing to run the risk.

Nadine looks into Mother Kralik's face. Whatever the old crone is yelling, it doesn't mean shit. When she looks into those filmy eyes, she sees herself, emotionless.

"Glyaahhh glyaaahh brrrhaaaa," Mother Kralik says, her serpentine tongue waggling like a tentacle. Her gums are bloody and her breath is putrid. Her liver is reeking inside her. She is a disease!

Vertigo! The tongue disappears and Yann appears, ramming his dick into her ass. Nadine's ass. It's an anemone. Yann fucks it with a harpoon. He fucks it until it turns into a mirror — the mirror in April's bedroom, where her reflection is stretching but her face remains the same. She is an infection! She is *shit!* She is *nothing!* Her father slaps her across the face, jams his finger into her ass. A rat scratches in her colon. Her father is a fudge man, slapping her up and beating her mother. There's shit on his dick and pubes in his teeth. Her mother's head bounces off the wall. So what? April and Suzanne dance in the cove. Their nudity is an atom bomb. April's pink is suicide . . .

"Haw haw haw haw haw haw! . . ."

Laughter! Mother Kralik's rancid laughter. The witch is

looking into her mind — her ticking twitching epileptic mind, which, now, is hearing this:

"And then you came back, oh yes you did! Maybe you don't remember, though, seeing as how you were all wigged-out and feverish! Oh yes, you were delirious! That's what you were, you little pussy licker! But did I object? Oh no, it'd been a long long time since anyone'd gone down on me! Haw haw haw! You crack me up, Nadine, the way you kept mumbling, 'April . . . April . . . April . . .' It was pitiful! *Haw!* It made me want to take a shit! Right in your mouth!"

"Huh?" Nadine asks, suddenly startled. She's starting to put two and two together.

"Yep!" Mother Kralik continues. "You were a pathetic sight, missy! Blubbering away like that — what the fuck is wrong with you?! But still, I obliged. Not that you made me come or nothing, but you did give me a good cleaning out. And believe me, there must've been a half ton of nasty crusty discharge in there! *Haw haw haw!*"

Nadine stares agape at Mother Kralik. Her jaw is actually hanging open.

"But you wouldn't stop blubbering, you disgusting little dyke! All that rank yellow rot — you just kept sucking it up! It was enough to gross even me out. That's why I had to start smacking you in the ears! But that just made you get off even more, now, didn't it?!"

Nadine can't take it. She breaks from her state and slaps Mother Kralik in the face. A tooth goes flying across the room.

"Devil whore!" Mother Kralik screams. "That was my last toof!"

The room is shocked into silence.

"Now you've really gone and done it!" Mother Kralik snarls, grabbing the golden crucifix and shaking it at Nadine. "You filthy little lesbian! You syphilis scab! You gonorrhea pustule! You're dead, bitch, you're fucking dead!"

Mother Kralik's eyes bulge wide, then roll back in her head. To Nadine it appears as if her orbs have been replaced by two peeled hard-boiled eggs. Mother Kralik mumbles stuff, swaying around like a puppet, invisible strings jerking her limbs. The room spins.

Nadine looks at her mother. Her mother is a drooling fool, and the hags are worthless imbeciles, muttering like monks to save themselves. They're terrified, the stupid old biddies!

"Be damned, you cum-sucking slut!" Mother Kralik screams, her eyes now back in their sockets. *"For now I cast my curse upon thee, devil whore! And your precious little rich bitch! You're DEAD!"*

"Now see what you've done," Nadine's mother suddenly says, breaking from her catatonic stupor, "you little idiot!"

Nadine flips out, breaks everything in flailing distance, slaps at her back as if she's covered with biting flies, then springs for Mother Kralik — to wring her motherfucking neck.

"YIIIIII-YIIIIIIII-YIIIIIIIIIIIIIIII!" screams Nadine, as her mother gets in front of her and holds her back. Nadine claws at the air, and then her mother's face — screeching like a bevy of slaughterhouse swine.

"YIIIIIIIIIIIIII! YIIIIIIIII-IIIIIIIIII-IIIIIIIIII!"

"You'd be better off taking on your Hollywood whore,

devil bitch!" Mother Kralik advises Nadine. "But you're afraid of her! You're her little scrub slut! That's what you are! She's got you in her spell!"

"Me?!" Nadine is surprised to hear herself say — having given up on the idea of language. "Afraid of her?!"

"Yes!" Mother Kralik shoots back, her breath a blast of septic miasma. "You wash her feet, you wash her ass, you wash Yann's cum out of her shithole!"

"I'll show you!" Nadine replies. "I'll wash her mother-fucking soul! That's what I'll do! The *bitch!* I'll show you, bitch! I'll show the *whole bitch world!*"

And off they go, all of them, following Nadine into the storm.

28

FATHER O FLUGENCE KNOWS there's nothing he
can do. It's all in the hands of God now, or the
Devil — who can tell the difference? The latter, of
course, knows these people better.

Father O'Flugence, however, believes in God no more
than he believes in the Devil — he knows it's just an excuse
for a job. What he does believe in is *fraternity* — but he
knows he's in the wrong place for this. The island is an
atrocity, its people are an abomination, and its future is just
the same as its past: disaster. He closes his shutters, lets the
storm hammer at his house, and pretends to pray.

He appeals to Nature to exterminate those who deserve
it. Mother Kralik is at the top of his list — a fact that he is
ashamed to admit but, nevertheless, confesses. He is evil
and he knows it. He hates. He hates her and the women of
the island. He hates the way they look, he hates the way
they think. He hates the way they walk, the way they chew
their food, the sound of their voices, their insignificant
concerns — everything they do. He hates them all. Except

Nadine . . . such a dear child . . . the only hope for their gender on the island. April, of course, won't last long.

Father O'Flugence believes in Nature. He believes it has a mind of its own, but no destination. He believes that humans evolved from primates, and that some are still apes. He believes we are all part of a big mistake, that the species is corrupt, and that the storm is pure. He believes that Nature is correcting itself. He believes that accidents are glorious, and that the will of Nature is the only will.

"Do what you will, Will," he pleads to the darkness, "but please spare the young lads . . ."

Meanwhile, Mother Kralik rages through the storm, working the women up. "Slaughter the whore!" she screams, jabbing her cross at the sky. "Burn the whore! Tear her limb from limb! Rip her fucking cunt wide open!"

"Rip her fucking cunt wide open!" the hags repeat. "Rip her fucking cunt wide open!"

Now there are even more than before. They've emerged from the woodwork — coming from kitchens, trailers, the night shift at the factory. There are at least two dozen of them, brandishing sticks, stones, fireplace pokers, rope. Leaning into the downpour, carving a path with swipes and swats, their intentions clear and venomous as they head up the hill toward April's house like a pack of skinheads on their way to an immigrant picnic.

"I'll spit in her face, that stinking bitch!" Nadine lets them know. "I'll rip her motherfucking ovaries out! I'll take care of her! That California movie bitch! I'll rip her goddamn gallbladder out!"

They arrive at April's house. Mother Kralik walks right up to the front door, shatters the window with the crucifix, reaches in, and turns the bolt. Nadine pushes past, and they all burst in with the storm.

"What was that?" Suzanne asks. She can feel the storm on the roof and all the walls of the house.

"What's what?" April asks groggily. She is still hugging Suzanne from behind.

Then they feel the footsteps on the stairs. A stomping sound is coming closer — many stomping sounds. They sit up in bed, the door bursts open, and the hags come screeching in.

Suzanne screams. April screams. The hags scream. For almost half a minute, everybody screams. Nadine flicks on the lights, and all of them continue to scream as their eyes adjust. Then, when April and Suzanne recognize their tormentors, they scream even louder, which causes the hags to scream back harder.

"What do you want?!" April manages to gasp, but nobody answers. Nadine drags her out of bed. She shoves her up against the wall.

"You cunt! You slut! You devil whore!" Nadine screeches, off her rocker. "You stinking semen-sucking bitch!"

April doesn't know how to respond. She just shakes her head, denying the crime as Nadine looks her up and down like a piece of meat, then spits in her face.

"Filthy fucking hosebag whore!" Nadine gouges with her tongue. "Why'd you come here?! Come on, tell me! You can't say, huh? You bitch! You smear of shit! You crab-infested dog-fucking whore! You should've stayed where you came from! From the Devil! Well I'm the Devil, too, and I'm gonna do a makeup job on you! So get ready to marry the devil!"

The hags grab hold of April. Nadine goes to the dressing table and brings back a handful of cosmetics. She smears lipstick all over April's mouth. The hags squeal hysterically, pinching and twisting April's skin.

"You look like a clown!" Nadine laughs. "Hey, where's the circus at?!"

April screams again as Mother Kralik steps forward and slaps her in the face. April turns away, and when she does Mother Kralik rolls her over and lifts her nightgown up, revealing her ass. Mother Kralik gets down on her knees and bites her on the butt, twisting her jaws back and forth like a feeding shark. April screams again as Mother Kralik rolls her back, spitting a wad of meat in her face.

"You've got nice wide eyes, huh?" Nadine asks. "Come on, tell me, you sack of shit! You sleazy slut! You've got nice wide eyes, don'tchya?! Yeah, the wide eyes of a trashy little whore! And the smelly tits of a dirty stinky lesbian, that's what you got! . . . But your tits ain't big! You ain't got big tits! Oh no! You got little tits! You got itty-bitty titties, that's what you got! And zits! And an ugly black snatch! And Yann don't give a shit for you! And you ain't preggy! You ain't shit! You're nothing! Do you hear me?! Nothing! You're shit!"

April stares aghast at Nadine, too afraid to say anything. There's a puddle of blood under her ass. She'll never wear a bikini again.

"But we're gonna start with your eyes!" Nadine screeches. "I'm gonna give you some little pisshole eyes, you stool-sucking bitch-cunt-whore! Hold her still!"

April suddenly breaks away. She scrambles for the door, but the hags tackle her and hold her head against the bed. Nadine approaches with a needle and thread — her hair gone wild like that of some mad composer just out of bed.

"I'm gonna sew your eyes shut!" Nadine informs April. "You goddamn member of the itty-bitty titty committee!"

The hags, however, have forgotten about Suzanne, who has just emptied her bladder on the bed, before recalling the flare gun. She reaches down, finds it, points it at Nadine, and pulls the trigger. *Bllaff!* There's smoke as the flare enters her abdomen. Nadine falls back against the makeup table and looks down. There's a big black hole in her stomach, and flames are shooting out.

"AIIIIIIIEEEEEE!" Nadine screams and tries to cover it up, but the shower of sparks burns at her hands. The women shield their eyes as the room grows even brighter. It burns for over a minute, blazing orange all over the place.

And then it fizzles, and so does Nadine. She drops to the floor, and the rupture in her belly gives birth to her intestines. Her dress is up around her waist, and her crotch is exposed. She is bleeding from her vagina, her period having finally arrived. Everyone is silent.

But then the shrews shriek with fury. They charge Suzanne and grab the gun away from her. They rip off her nightgown and beat her senseless. And then they do the same to April. In the end, two naked women are lying on top of Nadine as the hags take turns kicking them.

"Now do you see what happens to whores who come here without an invitation!" Mother Kralik snaps at April. "We never wanted your pretty ass here, miss rich bitch! You're a disease here, you disgusting little slut! With your big fat tits and your million-dollar movie muff! You came to the wrong place! Oh yes! You came to the place where dog food rules! That's right! We're humanity gone bad, baby! That's who we are! We're what's left after the gutting's been done! We're a bucket of fish heads and blood! All of us! We're worse than scum! *We're chum!!!* . . . And you stepped in it!"

April tries to object, but Mother Kralik slaps her in the mouth. April gulps. She knows her ass is grass.

"Oh!" Mother Kralik responds. "I'm soooo sorry, dear, did I smear your makeup? Hmmmm . . . you don't look so pretty anymore . . . In fact, you look kinda flushed! I think you could use a powder!"

Mother Kralik grabs all the perfumes and powders she can find and pours them on April and Suzanne. She laughs at them, then lifts up her skirt and positions her wrinkly old ass in front of their faces.

For a second, April can see Mother Kralik's ancient organ — like a mess of hissing, twisting serpents, tangled in a thinning thicket, all surrounding a crusted yellow hole — which suddenly widens. Mother Kralik pisses on them as the women roar approvingly.

"Please," April begs, "she's just a girl, let her go, please . . ."

"Shaddap!" Mother Kralik orally defecates — then shoves the crucifix under April's nose.

"You want this?!" Mother Kralik demands.

April nods yes.

"Well you're gonna get it!" She laughs. "Oh yes, you're gonna get it! You're gonna get it good!"

Then . . .

####################################
#####################################
#####################################
#####################################
################################.
"#####################################!"
"#####################################!"
####################################
#####################################
#####################################
#############################.
[CENSORED]
####################################
#####################################
#####################################
###########################.
"######################################
###########!"
"########################!"
"###############################?!"
"#####################!..."
#####################################
#####################################
#####################################
#####################################
#####################################
###############################...

####################################
#####################################
#####################################
###############################...

After April and Suzanne have been thoroughly violated, Mother Kralik leads her legion back to the storm — holding the cross high in the sky. April and Suzanne have been tied together naked.

"To the cliffs!" Mother Kralik cries. "To the cliffs!"

The storm thunders and flashes. April and Suzanne are hauled to the bluff. The ocean is smashing at the talus below. Megatons crash and bash, going off like bombs. Chaos in the sky, anarchy in the sea. Calamity!

The hags are squealing, drunk on blood. They set their cargo near the edge. Mother Kralik walks up and looks at them. Suzanne has fainted, but April hasn't. She is shivering, and begging again — a trait which Mother Kralik has become quite bored with.

"Can't you do any better?" Mother Kralik asks.

But she can't. April continues to blubber away.

"Come on!" Mother Kralik coaxes. "Say something! It'll be your last chance ever!"

". . . poo-poo . . ." April finally manages to whisper.

Mother Kralik rolls her eyeballs in annoyance, steps up, and kicks the bundle over the edge. The violence of the tempest drowns out April's cry.

"Send us a postcard, bitch!" Mother Kralik screams.

The pink mass hits the rocks, bounces once, and disappears into the foaming spraying turbulence below.

"Oh well," Mother Kralik tells the women, and shrugs. She takes out a pack of Tic Tacs, which she found in April's purse, pops one in her mouth, and inquires of the ladies, "Mint . . . anyone?"

Widow Flanahan steps up, and Widow Murphy after her. They divvy up the candy, then head back to town.

29

B Y DAWN IT S CALM, and the ships are twenty-seven miles out, injured but still afloat. Three of them have weathered the storm. All flags fly at half-mast, except on one. Yann's boat. Where the mainmast is missing.

Charlie had done an excellent job of riding the waves. He rode one for over three miles before catching the next one. The other boats had followed suit, and the tempest eventually passed.

Now all the pumps are pumping away and the nets are being retrieved. They still have a couple of miles of nets left.

On Yann's boat, Charlie has appointed himself captain, with no objection from the crew. He saved their ass, he can have the crystal meth — if there's any left. The others just want to get back to the island.

The Big Run, however, is still on. They can see the salmon leaping and splashing, heading for freshwater. To go back without a catch is unheard of, even if there are dead onboard. They get to work restringing the nets.

A few hours later, the boats are chugging for shore, following the salmon back to the island's only stream. Tons of fish get snagged in the process, including rare white king and protected chinook.

Yann has been banished to the bilge, where the pumps are running steadily. He sticks his head up and looks around. It is sunny outside, and the gulls are gliding over the rail.

Yann looks toward the stern, where Lester and Fred are hoisting the captain's body over the edge — he hits the water like a sack of garbage, bobs a couple of times, and ends up shark food.

"And don't come back!" Charlie calls after him. The three of them laugh at the captain.

The fishermen still will not talk to Yann — unless it's to give him an order. His quick thinking may have saved them for a bit, but he is not one of them. This is their message to him, and he hears it loud and clear. Yann doubts he'll even get paid for this trip.

"Get the fuck back down in your hole!" Charlie yells at him, and he obeys, slinking back to the belly of the ship.

Periodically, the boats stop and haul in their nets, emptying their catches onto the decks. Down in Seattle this primo salmon would no doubt be prized, but up here it will be mixed with ratfish and manta. Nobody will ever know the sweet pink flesh gone to waste. By the time these fish arrive in Japan, they will be part of a brown gelatinous mass.

The nets are set again, and the boats continue on, hauling in every ten or fifteen minutes. The fish have become more concentrated now, though mostly they're only common dog salmon.

It is late in the afternoon, and the sun is getting lower. Charlie and Fred are drinking harder, Lester is already out. They won't make it another couple hours. Yann will have to drive the boat in. They decide to call him up from the hold.

"Hey, Fuckdick!"

Yann comes up and sees it in the distance, rising jagged, like the smoldering shoulders of some medieval demon: the island.

"Stop!" Charlie suddenly yells. "Stop the fucking winch!"

Fred cuts the power as they crowd around the pulleys, looking down. Yann walks over to see what they caught . . . probably a seal or something.

With all that ocean out there, the chances that April and Suzanne would end up in their nets were not very great. Still, the salmon could sense the freshwater flow, so that's where they were going. Which is why Yann's boat was where it was, as well as the corpses caught in the current.

So there they are: naked and bloated, bound with rope, and covered with yellowish purple bruises. The men haul them up, dump them out, and stare at their bare beaten bodies.

Yann gawks. He knows the face of April, even if it's hideous, with bulging eyes and a rigid grimace. Who the other woman is, though, he doesn't have a clue. But that doesn't matter. The only explanation is there is no explanation. That's the way it is — and he must accept it.

Yann doesn't know how to feel as he cuts the ropes away. He tries to make their bodies lie flat, but the stiffness has already set in — they are contorted, disfigured, bent beyond repair. Yann pushes down on them like he's trying to close an overstuffed suitcase. It doesn't work very well. Some bones get broken.

"Shit," he mutters. And then it hits him like a brick: April is dead, and beautiful no more. She's gone forever. Destroyed . . .

Yann separates the women and lays a tarp over each of them. The fishermen finish hauling in. Their boat is full.

"Yann!" Charlie calls. "You're driving!"

Yann gets up and goes to the wheel as Charlie goes around to the stern to pass out with Lester and Fred, snoring and farting in drunkenness. By the time they get to shore, they'll be sober enough to unload.

Yann rides into the glowing dusk, looking out across the forms lying supine on the deck. The squawking of the gulls eats at him. His gut begins to wrench.

He thinks of those lips — those lips which had formed the horizons and valleys of everything — the only reason he had to head back to the island, all the hope and strength in him. He thinks of those lips and sees them clearer than ever before, now that they are nevermore.

But they are. They exist. They're out there on the deck right now — and all he has to do is what he is driven to, before he can never do it. So he puts a bungie on the wheel and leaves the helm.

Kneeling down in front of her tarp, he peels it back a bit.

Her dead eyes stare up at him, veiled with a whitish film. And beneath them: those lips — transfigured, pulled back — her mouth frozen open, tongue puffed up inside.

Yann's eyes glaze. His breast beats erratically. Everything he loves in the world is gone. Yann stares and stares. And makes her lips beautiful again. They are beautiful for him.

He lowers his lips to hers. But when they get within an inch, he hesitates. No heat rises — he might as well just kiss a fish. But her lips are there — and he will be fulfilled, he will be able to keep on going, he will go to the redwoods, get himself a crabbing boat, find a substitute wife, spawn some kids, and forget . . .

He trembles, and lowers his lips a fraction of an inch. His lips are almost touching hers. He closes his eyes and aims his face — but can't. Something refuses.

Yann pulls back, gets up, staggers to the rail, and pukes. When he's through, he wipes his mouth and feels the pressure rising inside. He has to let it out: *"Fuuuuuuuuuuuuuuu-uucccccccccccccckkkkkkkkk!"* Yann howls, for the first time in his life. He wants to kill. He wants to die.

After a while the island looms larger. Yann covers April up and goes back to the wheel. The other boats are following, and the docks are approaching. It is sunset, and there are black forms standing silent on the slips, waiting to see who the widows will be.

The crew wake up and ready the ropes. Yann cuts the engine as they drift in. Wordlessly, the boat is tied to the pilings. Four men step off, one woman drops.

Yann feels the void envelop him. He might as well just be a ratfish, whose only purpose is to form a turd for some poodle in Japan. His worthlessness is the most profound thing about him.

He heads for the bar to get fucked up.

The island owes him this.

Meanwhile, out in the Bering Strait, the Coast Guard is coming up from Nome. Greenpeace has filed a complaint against the Alaskan fishing industry regarding the sale of Yukon salmon to the Russians. And the Alaskan fishing industry, in turn, has sent the U.S. government to find out what is going on.

There are questions to be answered, and men onboard to enforce the laws of the United States of America: policemen, detectives, even an agent of the FBI, who intends to question April. The media are also along for the ride.

The shit is about to hit the fan.

30

IN CHURCH, the women are on one side and the men are on the other. Yann and the Australian gent are among the men, and Mother Kralik and Widow Murphy are among the women. Father O'Flugence presides, three coffins beneath the pulpit.

Whatever is said makes no sense. Yann knows he will never leave the island — why the fuck should he? Happiness is selfishness, and monotony is reality. Like the island. Which he is part of. It's real. Too real. And he will never leave it.

Yann knows that the men will talk with him again, and that he will fish with them again, and drink with them again, and if he's lucky, grow old with them. He will carry on the ways of the island, and fish as Bubba did, and all the men before him did, for generations. He will live like them. And die like them, off the shores of the island. Northern California exists no more. He is resigned to this.

The night before he fucked a whore. He pretended she was Nadine, and was glad that she wouldn't shut up. The bitch just kept talking smut. It gave him the excuse to hit her. So he did. So what? And then he fucked her again, and didn't even use a rubber.

Yann sits there and sweats. He sweats like a fucking pig. He stinks. All night long he snorted crank. It felt good. He drank and drank. To become one of them. To ditch the fool he used to be. To get along on the island.

Then he went to the junk store. Through the glass he could see his accordion there. The money had already gone up his nose. He stared at it, the piece of shit! And for a second he almost wanted it back. What a dumbshit!

The priest blares on, talking in a monotone. He talks about the evil in women who lay together, and the misfortune that happens when citizens dare to take a stand for what's right. He talks about how innocents die when they try to keep sinners in line. He talks about tragedy, and coming together. He talks about "fraternity."

Father O'Flugence is on a roll. He talks about the depths of hell. How hell is having to live with monsters. How hell is having to see them take part of you, and merge it with themselves. How hell is a place that's easy to get to. And how hell becomes home. Blah, blah, blah . . .

Yann feels the need for a drink. To settle his nerves. To make him numb. To have in his hand. To put in his mouth. To lift up and down. To do something with.

The priest keeps droning on. He says some more religious things. It's the same stuff every time. He knows it all by heart, the sad old fucker.

Father O'Flugence gives the signal, and the organ starts to play. Music rises from the pipes — long, resonating notes that hold in the air. They're there in the air, almost solid.

Yann gets up. Everyone does. The whole church heads for the door.

Nadine's mother nods to Yann, and he nods back. The organ continues to hold its note. She doesn't look that bad for her age. She is still gazing at him. Another note rises from the pipes. Yann looks away, knowing what his look can do. A couple more like that, and she'll be knocking at his door. And maybe he'll let her in.

Widow Murphy follows him. When she gets outside, Mother Kralik is there. She's lighting a cig.

"Got another?" Widow Murphy asks, and Mother Kralik gives her one. They huddle together and get it lit.

Mother Kralik is strangely silent. She crosses herself and looks toward the sky. Actual tears form in her eyes. Widow Murphy shrugs, and the dirge begins.

In the graveyard, Yann takes his place in line and moves slowly through the overcast — April's casket on his shoulder. He mucks through the mud toward a pit someone dug, the postal clerk next to him, Charlie up front, and Hans at his side.

Gray rain falls from the gray shitty sky.

Meanwhile, half a mile away, spawning sockeye leap upstream, as silt and sperm mix with egg, as the flesh of the male starts to turn red, as the cycle continues — as it has for centuries — in the draining rains, rushing over rocks, running under logs, cascading down to the mouth of the stream, where debris fans out alluvially: granite slabs,

busted lava, crushed quartz, and other igneous conglomerations, carpeted by barnacles, covered with limpets and
starfish and urchin — and crabs, crawling from the cracks,
across the crevasse of chasms and fissures where wolf eels
wind and wait for their prey — in the rubble surrounding
the island.